The Realm of Angels

An Angel-tale by Fibby Bob Kinney
(With Poems and inspiration)
By
Fe Rosario Vergara-Maximo

Introduction:

This is my 17th. Book of poems and fairytales. Most of the stories and poems I have written fall into the category somewhere between child and adult. I never had a real audience for my writing as it was somewhere in the cracks of literature.

This book is different. I have found that my genre is a new slant on the fairytale... in this case, my stories are written for "the child in the adult."
The theme for this new Genre is (Passion With Innocence)...fBk)

A sort of, "Grown Up" fairytale, only in this case I'm calling it -" Angel-tales".
All the stories in this book deal with Angels as the main characters.

They take on the properties and dimensions of human beings. Only they have wings and can fly. A wish that the active imagination is fond of; and would love to give it a try if possible.
I ask you, the reader, to use your imagination and come along on this trip into a fantasy that has many twists and turns to it.

See the angels from the sky above and watch how they have to deal with the same problems and joys that we have to deal with as humans on our Earth.

I wrote the story and did the poems for the male angel in each chapter. My partner, who is from the Philippines, did the poems for the female angel. Our bio's and pictures are in the back of the book..along with some of the awards we received for parts of this story and others we individually did.

I hope you will enjoy the adventures of these angels as they travel through the many adventures they encounter on their way to find the fulfillment of their lives.
Please enjoy this first Angel-tale...fBk

Learning The Pen Mysteries
International Literary Platform

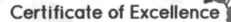

Certificate of Excellence

is graciously given to

Fibby Bob Kinney
Fe Rosario Vergara-Maximo

(USA & Philippines)

Poem's Title : My Dearest Flower
(A Collaboration)

for his/her excellent poem posted in
the week of Nov. 21-27, 2022

Given on Nov. 27, 2022

Founder,
Matthew Edeh

Administrative
Board Members

4

Table of Contents

Opening

The Realm of Angels
An Angel-tale by Fibby Bob Kinney
With poems and inspiration
By
Fe Rosario Vergara-Maximo

In the clouds above the real world there were two kingdoms of Angels. The moderate angels dream with the life forces on Earth. It is their job to tend to the lesser of good and evil. That is, they try to moderate the emotions of most beings on earth and keep them from going to any extremes in thought or deed.

The deep wish angels work with deep longing and erotic thoughts. It is their job to keep these thoughts and wishes from going too far in the entity that has them in their subconscious.

These two kingdoms of angels are not friendly with each other. As one is always looking to be in charge. Most of all, there is a fine line that separates the duties of the two. And this is where the problems arise. Which one should be the force that deals with the earthly entity and their thoughts?

So over eons of time the two kingdoms became totally independent of each other. To the point where if an angel in one kingdom was to try to mingle with one from the other side…the penalty was imprisonment.

Realm of Angels :Part 1
(The Two Angels)

Our story begins with two angels who defied the rules and became friends with each other …as there is a Portal in each castle window that allows them to see the other side. This is done so the angels can monitor each other and make sure that they are dealing correctly with the same entity on the Earth world.

Fabszy, the male from the extreme dream kingdom…and Rosie, the female angel from the moderate dream kingdom,

On this day, Fabszy chose to break the rules and he sent this poem by mechanical pigeon to the far off moderate kingdom. The mechanical pigeon flew into the tower window of her bedroom and deposited this poem in the hand of Angel Rosie… it read…

The Fountain of Love

Is there a source to the Fountain of Love?
One that comes down from heaven above?
To show that secret hidden place;
Where all sins in thought are erased.

To climb the mountain on slippery slope;
In the claim that there is divine hope.
To touch the stars at the mouth of the well;
The secret place where love does dwell.

Is there a marker on the road so long?
To show the spot where the well belongs?
A path through the endless terrain;
At its center this treasure to gain.

Beneath the trees that grow in depth,
An entrance to the cave is spent.
It hovers in a shimmering glow;
Where the treasure is buried below.

Ah, to reach this spot upon the ladder;
The rungs of which are made of matter.
But the well is dry to the naked eye;
As all who seek it find on first try.

It is only when the well itself is alive,
That the treasured love is found inside.
Let he or she be the chosen guide.
Find what love itself does hide.

The messenger of the angels choice;
Will find the glow and then rejoice.
As the manna of life is in pure hands;
Its fate and honor are its demands…
FIBBY Bob Kinney ©

She read the poem. A tear appeared in her
angel eyes. She knew she was about to break
the rules. But her desire overcame her fears
and she sent back her response:

There's a Fountain of Love
A belief in ancient times
That the fountain brings

Forth a powerful water
Where cupid dips his arrow
And shoots the hearts
Of man and woman he chooses
Or which lovers drink the
Magical water and fall in love.
Lovers then experience
The thrilling first beguiling
Moments of love.

I wish that we join together
In a journey in ardent search
Of this Fountain of Love
But I have my doubts
That the magical power
Of this liquid might no longer
Have a spell on aging hearts.
On second thoughts
and reflection , I realize
The Fountain of Love
You are looking for
Does have spring water
That never ceases its flow
Reaching everyone , regardless
Of age, color, and gender.

The Spring Water
To this Fountain of Love
Supplies endless love and grace

It quenches anyone who thirsts
Heals gaping wounds,
Like a divine balm, it soothes
Aches and unbearable pains.
It erases doubts and fears
It transforms weaknesses
It grows seeds of peace and trust
It conquers fears and hates
It floods to unite divisions
It washes away our sins
It makes us whiter than snow.
It sanctifies our souls
It transforms and restores
Broken bonds and relationships
It gives serenity and tranquility
It gives hope for life eternity.

I heard that it can be found here
And now; no need to climb a ladder
For the Wellspring has been dug deeper
Within our hearts .
Unfortunately, not all can find it so
For many who leave the narrow road
Make detour, tread the wider road
Are led astray, never finding
The Well that they've been seeking.
They will only find a dry well
Unless they yield to the One
Who will lead them to that Well

That never dries and never tastes stale.

So my good friend, together
We drink that Living Water
From the Fountain of Love
The source of which is from Above.
We'll generously share it with others
That they, too, may taste the wondrous ,
Endless grace of the Fountain of Love.fvvr
Fe Rosario Vergara-Maximo ©

Realm of Angels …. Part 2
(Imprisonment)

As soon as the magical pigeon flew back to the
extreme dream kingdom it dropped the poem
into Fabszy's lap. He watched as the pigeon
flew up to the top shelf of the bookcase that
was in his room. Then carefully he opened the
poem and read it completely.

A tiny tear filled his angel eyes. It was a
continuation of the poem he had sent to her.
He could picture her sweet angelic face as she

wrote these words with the golden quill that was the angel's choice of writing instruments. He realized he had to see her in person. To touch her wings, to feel her breath as she spoke to him. He would take this daring chance that was forbidden.

But first he would write a poem to her. He took his golden quill and dipped it in the glowing ink. The simmering ink produced a rainbow of colors. It would change its color to fit the emotions of the words that the poem expressed. Bright blue for happy feelings. Green to express the wealth of Nature. Yellow for the serenity of the Sun's rays. Red for the emotional deep feeling of passion and love. The poem would come alive as it was read and it reached out to touch the feelings of the reader. He took the quill in his angelic hand and began the poem:

Your Aura

I can sniff the sweet scent of your aura,
From the words I whisper upon this page.
So distinct is its honey that all my senses it does engage.
It rings a chime to my ears as a breath's sage.

What distant heartbeat is this to my ear?
So far away, yet to me so near.
A dreaming Angel that tickles my wit,
With me always, as I stand or I sit.

So sweet is the scent of a dreaming land;
Where wild bushes grow upon command.
Mountains of smooth silky creamy touch;
Calling to the bare senses so much.

An abandoned safety to explore the deep;
Into caverns the brave must creep.
To find the honeyed treasure galore,
And seek its mystery to adore.

Honey and roses together as one;
To kneel and cuddle as prayer is done.
Let the scroll of your body be written in charm;
All of it precious and free from harm…

Let my thoughts fly into your sleep.
To cover you completely and deep.
Upon the wings of wishes my wants abide;
From my seeking no part of you can hide.
Fibby Bob Kinney ©

As soon as he finished the poem he attacked it
to the leg of the magical pigeon.

It flew directly to the castle window of Rosie the moderate angel.

She took it immediately in her soft hands and read it completely. She was overjoyed by its content, still, she feared that Fabszy might do something foolish and try to fly to her kingdom.

Her fear was well founded. As a moderate guardian angel had seen the pigeon fly into her turret window. He put the soldier angels on alert. They would watch the clouds carefully to make sure no angel from the extreme dream kingdom didn't break the rules and try to fly to the moderate dream land.

Then late that night it happened. An angel with dark wings flew through the night clouds and entered the bedroom turret window of Rosie the moderate angel.

As soon as she saw him she wrapped her wings around him and they kissed deeply. Then she pulled away and said, "Oh No, you must not be here. Your angel's life is in danger. You have broken the rules."

Fabszy's angelic face glowed as he said, "My darling, you are worth the risk. I had to see you, to be close to you, to touch you" With that said, he enclosed her in his wings and kissed her deeply. She could not refuse him.

In the midst of their kiss the door of Rosie's turret room burst open. Two soldier angels swooped in and ripped Fabszy from their embrace and hauled him out of the room.

When he was gone the Archangel came in and spoke to Rosie. "It was not your fault that this dark angel came to you. He will be punished severely. You must forget this ever happened. As he is now lost to our dungeon,forever."..he left abruptly and Rosie was there with only her tears as company.

She finally composed herself and sat at the writing table in her room. She took her golden quill pen and said to herself. "I shall write a poem to Fabszy to tell him of my sorrow for what has happened to him. I will tell him of my inner desires. Then I will find a way to set him free from that dark dungeon that holds him hostage. I will find a way to free him. With

those thoughts hovering in her mind she took
her pen and began to write…..

It had been two days since the soldier angels
had ripped Fabszy from Rosie's arms. He was
lost in the dungeon in the depths of the
moderate dream castle.
Rosie felt in her angel heart that she must get
this poem that she wrote to him tonight or he
would die in that lonely dungeon.

With caution she descended the long spiral
staircase that led to the basement catacombs
of the castle. Carefully, she glided down the
dark corridors till she saw a faint light at the
dungeon door.

Stationed at the front of the iron door was a
soldier angel. As soon as he saw Rosie he
sprang to attention. He muttered the
words.."dear Angel, you must not be here. It is
forbidden to see or talk to the prisoner."

Rosie smiled and touched the shoulder of the
guard gently and said, "I am here to talk to this
Angel prisoner. Please let me pass.

The soldier angel, as if in a trance, took the skeleton key from around his neck and handed it to Rosie. He then bowed his head and drifted away.

Rosie opened the padlock and the iron door creaked open. She was horrified to see Fabszy laying in a heap in the corner of the room. He had no food or water for two days. His lips were parched and he was very weak from lack of food.

Rosie knelt beside him and cuddled him in her arms. He opened his eyes and gave a faint smile on his face.

Rosie with a slight blush said in a calming voice. I know you are dying of thirst and hunger. I must tell you my job on Earth is to feed hungry and starving children. Those that are trapped in poverty. I am a nursing Angel. I fly to them in their sleep and nurse then with my Angel breast milk. This is my duty to help the poor children and bring some heavenly nourishment to them.

She smiled softly. All I can do is offer you my breast to nurse you back to health. With that said, she cuddled Fabszy as a new born child and nursed him back to life.

Fabszy just couldn't pull himself away from her…he drank her dry. She was at the verge of passing out but did not refuse him. Finally, he realized he had gone too far and pulled his mouth from her breast. She swooned and said, "I have given you back your life. Now you must go. My duty is done."…but first this is the poem I have written to you"

With her soft angelic fingers glowing in the warmth of her body heat she handed the poem to Fabszy. He opened the scroll parchment and read her poem aloud:

Love's Lament:
When the sky's lighted by the full moon ,
You come to me in my lonely room
Your angelic face appears vividly
And I feel your masculine energy.

I must tell you now
That I've always liked you
I watched you from a distance
Flying above layers of clouds
Followed by other female angels

Their adoration made me jealous.

We'll, fly away on the wings of love
Down on earth where mortals hide in
Their secret cove
Where storms full trust can't remove
This feeling of abandoned desire
How enviable mortals are?
They have the freedom to love.
Sometimes I wish we were mortals
I would live with you to serve you
To make you happy .

Will songs be meaningful without you?
Will the music from the harp lull me to sleep?
I keep tossing in bed , you are all in my mind.
How I long to be with you.
To feel your fingers run through my hair
To feel you caress my face
To cuddle me in your arms.
To feel your burning lips on mine
To be peaceful as I sleep on your chest

In my dreams we fly above the clouds
Hand in hand, laughing and frolicking
The dark clouds tend to disappear
Only your words gladden me
Only your sweet smiles brighten my day

From a distance I admired you
I can't understand why despite our distance
I could I hear you play your violin
I could hear you sing a lonely lovesong
That resonates with my melancholic voice.

I can no longer endure this abysmal loneliness
I had to come to your dungeon
And put a soothing balm on your wounds.
I weep as I think about how you're suffering.
What is the use of living here
If I am not with you
You are now my everything.

I will refuse to dance and sing
I will not play the harp and the violin
As long as you are in chains.
Why must there be obstacles to true love?
Why must happiness turn to pains
And sufferings?

Love should not be nipped in the bud.
Every love must grow in full blossom.
Every love must shed its sweetness and
fragrance
Such will be our love.
I shall be your Rosie- The sweetest of Angels.
(Fe Rosario Vergara-Maximo (c)

After she read the poem aloud he wept. Fabszy stood up tall and straight and bowed to the kneeling Rosie... then he said two words..."Thank You"...He turned and with the power in his dark wings..he spread the iron bars on the cell window...his parting words were:

"As much as I love you, my loyalty to my kingdom keeps me from abandoning it. I must go back. But I leave my dearest dream with you" . Then he opened his dark wings and flew into the night.

Rosie, gathered herself together. She left the cell and handed the skeleton key to the soldier angel who was back on station. He took the key without a word.

In the early morning Golden Dawn the Sun arose upon the two kingdoms... Now, back as they were before...the forbidden love was gone. Vanished as a cloud of butterflies in the crisp air, but the dream that they had shared together, would last forever ...

Realm of Angels: part 3
(The Parting)

Fabszy flew through the night. His dark wings cut through the clouds at a feverish pitch. The Moon with an imagined grin upon its face peered down and lit the way back to the deep thought kingdom.

"How could it be?" His mind was in a flux of images. He remembered the meeting with Rosie the Angel of light. They had kissed and then the soldier angels ripped him from her arms. They punished him in a dungeon prison. He would have died had it not been for Rosie, who was a nursing Angel to the children of the needy on Earth. He remembered being parched without food or water. She placed her nursing breast in his mouth and gave him life. He suckled upon her until his strength returned. Then, she bid him farewell…as their romance was doomed. He, from the realm of the dark angels..and she is a pure Angel of mercy's grace. Yet, somehow they found a bond together. A love so deep it spanned beyond good and evil..in its purity of true compassion for each other.

He flew all the way home with tears in his eyes. Finally there was the gate to the dark kingdom. The gargoyle with bows at the ready recognized Fabszy and bowed to him as he entered the gate.

He flew up to the window in his tower room. It was still partially open and he swooped inside the comfort of his lodging.

For a long time he just lay there upon the silken sheets of his king size bed. Finally, he sat up. His wings still dripped a fine sweat from their exertion of the long flight. He moved to the comfort of his easy chair and felt deeply serene in its soft leather grip.

Then he leaned over and grasped the top of his oak desk. It was covered in carved etchings of flowers and little animals in play.

He took his Quilled pen in hand and began to write a poem to Rosie. It began, "Dearest Rosie, my nursing Angel of healing beauty. I know this is forbidden but I must write a poem to you. You saved my life with your breast milk..I can never forget the courage it took for you to do that to save me. I must write this poem to you. If in your heart you still care for me, even a little, then respond with a poem of your own.
Here are my thoughts about you."

He took the pen in his angelic hand and wrote
this poem.

A Taste of Honey

The thought of you is as a taste of honey to my
senses.
It drips as golden drops upon my brain.
So much of you in envisioned sight,
To pound my heart as a drum in delight.

The nearness of your breath is like a rose filled
garden.
So sweet the petals of your lips.
To touch your tongue tip with my own;
To feel the warmth of you as my home.

Such surprise in the curving of your hips;
As they dance upon your body.
You walk in measured steps,
As a graceful lioness in prey.

So subtle is the hint of your breasts:
The curvature beneath a blouse of silk.
The heated muscle tone of your arms,
Such delight becomes a beckoning charm.

The texture of your twinkling toes,

In leather sandals hugging in grip.
Your legs long and true to form;
As a dancer upon a concert trip.

The curve of your smile ripples down your
frame.
Such perfect precious movements engage.
The joining of hip and torso entwined;
As a flowery tree searchers a blooming vine.

My call to duty is your command.
Upon your word is my demand.
To fill your needs full and strong;
It is in your honor where I belong…
(Fibby Bob Kinney (c)

He finished the poem and attached it as a
scroll to the leg of the magical pigeon that was
the liaison between the two kingdoms. It would
fly through the dark clouds till it found the Sun
filled kingdom of the helping Angels. The ones
that stood for the wishful dreams.
The ones that protected the poor and the
innocent….far removed from Fabszy's realm,
yet there was a bond there between them.

The pigeon flew into the tower window of
Rosie's bedroom and dropped the note on her
lap. She opened the scroll and read its

contents. Tears flooded her eyes. She was in a flutter of mixed emotions. She flung herself to her bed and sobbed into the night.

She awoke when the voyeur moon peeked its glowing light into her darkened room. She had not visited Earth that day. Her angelic breasts were filled to the brim with the nursing milk she needed to deliver to the hungry children. They were swollen and hurt her to be free of this life giving milk.

All she could think of at that moment was Fabszy. How much she missed him. How she had fed him back from death's door. Oh, if he were only here now. She would feed him again. This time with her love intact. Then, she looked up and saw the magical pigeon was still there. It sat as a sentry on the top of her oak dresser. It waited obediently for her to write a poem in response to Fabszy…she sensed this and she obeyed her inner emotions. She took her peacock feathered pen and wrote this poem…

LET ME BE

Let me be your lucky charm
And you will be safe from harm.

Let me be your soft bed
On which to lay your head

Let me be your morning coffee
Or your afternoon cup of tea

Let me be your morning song
You happily sing all day long

Let me be your sunshine
And never will you whine

Let me be your glass of wine
That your lips may touch divine

Let me be your warm light
To keep you warm at night

Let me be your sweet water
And never will you feel bitter

Let me be your meal
That gives you the fill

Let me be your rainbow
And you will always be aglow

Let me be your sweet rose
And you will never feel cross

Let me be your blue moon
As you dreamily swoon

Let me be the rolling waves
That smoothen your rough edges

Let me be your summer and spring
Feeling young and gay, your keeping

Let me be your treasured book
You read in your cozy nook

Let me be your first
And let me be your last

Let me be your favorite thing
Oh, let me be your everything!

(Fe Rosario Vergara -Maximo (c)

Rosie finished the poem and attached it as a
scroll to the leg of the mechanical pigeon. It
immediately flew out the window of her tower
room and headed into the dark clouds that
were the domain of the deep thought kingdom.

The pigeon flew fast and gracefully as it darted
through the clouds. Still, there was a storm that

filled the night. Rain and thunder bellowed as the little bird flew on its journey. Then when it was within sight of Fabszy's turret window a bolt of lightning crackled and hit the bird head on.

All its mechanical works stopped churning and it plummeted to the Earth below. It lay embedded upon the rocks at the summit of the Enchanted mountain. The place on Earth that was a a meeting ground between fantasy and reality. The place where angels and mythical beasts tread to fulfill longing dreams. The pigeon was lost there with no way to escape. Only a miracle could help it finish its mission now...fBk

The Realm of Angels...part 4
(The Hidden Door)

The next morning after the storm had passed Fabszy awoke with a troubled look on his face. He knew the mechanical pigeon should have returned to him a long time ago. He knew the storm was strong but so was that pigeon. What could have happened to it?

Then the realization hit him. The pigeon was made of metal. Yes it was very strong and could stand high winds, but not a bolt of lightning.

Fabszy sprang from his bed. He looked from his tower window straight down. He could make out beneath the clouds the peak of the Sacred mountain. This was a strange and mysterious place. Even the angels were forbidden to go there. It was governed by a higher power than even the angels were in awe of. As this was the realm between fantasy and reality.

It was off limits to the angels of the two kingdoms who only dealt with the needs of the humans who inhabited the Earth. Now he was sure that the pigeon must have fallen there during the storm. He would break the rules once again, and fly into this magical kingdom himself..and find that pigeon who surely carried a poem from the pen of Rosie the sweet Angel.

Without another thought he dove out of the window and flew to the mountain below. He landed in the forest. At first, he was amazed. This was a beautiful forest full of swaying trees.

Some were weeping willows as they quietly sobbed in the light breeze of the fresh air. There were flower gardens everywhere. Birds and butterflies flew freely in the serene beauty of the magical forest.

As he walked through the lush gardens of greenery he saw a glint of metal on the rocks nearby. He rushed over and saw the mechanical pigeon moaning on the ground. He picked it up and clutched it in his angelic fingers.

This was all it needed to regain its powers. The pigeon purred and offered its foot to Fabszy. He took the scroll tied to the pigeon foot and read it aloud.

MUST I DEFINE LOVE?

To Fabszy:
I am trying to define love,
Do I need to?
Did you not see it in my eyes?
Did you not feel it when I gently tapped your shoulder?
Can you not feel the trembling of my hands when I write this poem?

Can you not hear the yearning of my love
songs from so far away?
Can you not feel my sadness when you keep
your silence ?
Can't you count how many times I have
forgiven you?
Can't you notice my joy when I kiss the poem
you have sent to me?
Or when I pluck a flower and put it on top of
your written words?
Can you not see how painstakingly I long for
the memory of you?

Can you not see how love is when I often blush
to think of it.
You are a glass of water to quench my thirst ?
Can you not feel its flavor when I drink it?
I can imagine your contentment when you
cuddle me?
Can you not see my tears that I miss you?
Can you not hear the lilting of my voice when I
call your name?
Can't you feel how I quiver when I dream of
your touch to me?
Can't you see how I feel about you.
kissing your poem even without your presence
?
Can't you feel love when I express my
repetitive thanks for your endless kindness?

Beloved, I need not define love.
Rely not on my words but
Rely on my tangible love...

All the little thousand things that make
you happy and sad define love.

(Fe Rosario Vergara- Maximo (c)

Fabszy read the poem and tears fell from his eyes. The teardrop fell upon the words of the poem and the ink absorbed them. The words upon the parchment paper began to shiver with him..they cried with their longing for him. It was her words and his tears in a dance of love..as they melted together upon the bed of the parchment paper.
Words and tears upon the bed of love.
He lifted the poem to his lips and kissed it gently. Then he threw himself upon the ground and moaned for her in longing.

Back at the moderate Angel Castle Rosie had made up her mind. She had not heard from Fabszy and she knew he would not venture to come to her as it would be his doom to do so. She decided she would go to him. Even though this was against all the rules she was taught as a good Angel, this was different. She felt a love in her heart like she hadn't known before. It was the need to be touched, to be thrilled by another Angel. One she could be close to, one that would accept her fears and joys, one that would share their longings with. She wanted to be near Fabszy, to touch him, and let him touch her.

With her mind made up she flew out of her tower bedroom window into the dark clouds ahead.

Fabszy finally stopped his tears. Rosie's poem still clutched in his fingers. He opened the scroll, and upon the back of the parchment he took his golden nibbed pen and began to write his poem to her…

Remembering You

Dearest Rosie:
I shall in my heart always know,
The kiss upon me you did bestow.
Not in the longing of carnal desire,
But to touch a source from much higher.

So gentle was our first kiss;
Nothing about it was amiss.

You touched my heart as a wand;
Flung by a cherub from beyond.

So natural and sweet is your touch.
I long to hold your hand so much.
Just to be near you is my want,
To awaken my dreams from a haunt.

You are a virgin Angel of pure breed.
Your goodness is what I need…
To shun the darkness within myself,
And put my bad qualities on a shelf.

Let me come to you in my thought,
As goodness to me you have brought.
I say this from my beating heart's desire;
For you to love me is all I require…
(Fibby Bob Kinney (c)

After he finished the poem he rolled it up in a tight knot and put it in the pouch on the magical pigeon's foot. He whispered to the pigeon…"take my poem to Rosie!" The bird obeyed and flew up into the dark clouds to complete its journey.

Rosie, who was flying in the clouds at that moment, saw the pigeon and bid it near. She took the poem from its leg and read it as she flew closer to the secret mountain. Then through an opening in the clouds she saw Fabszy down below. She zoomed down and flew right into his arms.

Their kiss was as deep and as passionate as could be imagined. Caution was forgotten, all that mattered was to be in each other's arms with love as the victor.

In the midst of their embrace a band of angels flew down from the sky. They pulled Rosie from his grip. They forced Fabszy to the ground and put chains on his arms and ankles. He lay there helpless in a kneeling position.

The Archangel from the moderate kingdom spoke directly to both of them.
He began.

"Angel Rosie, our sentry guard saw the pigeon fly into your turret window. He warned us and we followed you here. You have broken the rules and now you must pay dearly for your disobedience.
First we shall deal with this Angel from the deep kingdom."

He turned to Fabszy… and said, "you have been warned once..now action is necessary."

With that said he took a pair of flaming shears from the backpack he carried. He raised the shears and said. "An Angel carries the power of flight in their wingtips. With your wingtips gone you will be powerless to fly. You will be doomed to walk the earth with dead wings upon your back. They will be the burden you must carry as you walk endlessly through the forest…as you are a doomed being by your own undoing desires."

With that said, he swooped down and cut the wingtips off of Fabszy's once fabulous wings…now they lay useless on his back. No longer a regal stance of an Angel but a dead weight to carry for the rest of his life.

He looked up from his still kneeling position and said to the archangel.

"All I did was for love. You have robbed me of my precious gift of angel wings. I suffer now…but my Love for Rosie will be in my heart forever. Please, I beg you. Do not punish her, let me carry her burden of guilt. None of this was her fault. She is innocent..please forgive her!"

The Archangel looked directly at Fabszy and said…"I cannot forgive her..she broke the rules and must be punished severely for that."

With those words said, " the soldier angels grabbed Rosie and they all flew off into the ominous clouds that hung high in the sky.

Fabszy was left alone there on the ground. The chains had fallen off as his punishment was in the weight of the dead wings he carried on his back. He stood and looked around. There at the edge of the great forest was a hidden doorway.

He walked up to it. Noting how hard it was to walk upon the Earth with the dead weight of broken wings he now carried upon his back. As he approached the doorway which was shimmering in a golden light, he noticed a writing above the door that said, "Let all ye who wish to enter find the true, and only way."

Fabszy said to himself..it is up to me now to discover the secret of that doorway. I am still an Angel with my wits and magical thoughts..I shall find the secret ..as I must somehow free Rosie from her innocent sins of exploring love's wishes…

The Realm of Angels…part 5
(The Message)

Fabszy, his wings now useless lay as dead weight upon his back. The archangel from the Moderate Kingdom had cut off his wingtips with those flaming shears. The scissor blades had left him in a hopeless situation… he was doomed to roam the forest of this strange mountain till he could find a way through that hidden doorway that led to the interior of the land beyond.

Most of all, he was terrified to think of what might happen to Rosie. Those soldier angels took her back to the Moderate Kingdom. That archangel in charge threatened punishment for her because she disobeyed the rules and followed Fabszy to this magical realm.

After wandering around in a never ending circle Fabszy sat down to rest. He did find one very interesting thing. It was a wishing well. Right behind some tall bushes, invisible at first, he finally found it.

The well was made of mason stone. It had a canopy of tile slats that covered it like an umbrella. There was a crystal bucket on a golden chain that could be lowered into the well.

Fabszy hadn't eaten or drank all day and he was famished. He cranked the bucket down into the well and when he raised it back up it was full of fresh well water.
He took a long drink from the crystal bucket which felt like a large goblet in his hands.

The water was fresh and cool. It had a life giving effect to it. Immediately he felt the presence of the magic water in his body. It didn't give him any special powers but it did satisfy his hunger and thirst. He surmised that this well was there for the travelers who got trapped in these woods. Without this magic water they would die of hunger and thirst while they searched to find a way to enter that hidden doorway.

Then he noticed all around the well there were piles of bones. Skeletons of those who sought the secret to the magic kingdom and failed. He surmised there must be a time limit on how long one could search before they gave up in frustration and lay down to eternal sleep. He made up his mind that this would not happen to him. He used to be a virile Angel with many resources to rely upon. Yes, now his wings were just a burden but he still had his wits about him.

The mechanical pigeon flew over and landed on his shoulder. He reached up and patted its wire feathers and said, "at least I still have you"

Then, he took his plume pen and paper and began to write a poem to Rosie.

To My Enchanted Angel

My dearest darling of winged desire,
My love for you grows higher and higher.
It matters not that my wings are gone,
Your love in my heart is where It belongs.

I will find a way to enter the place;
The magic doorway can't be erased.

It is up to me to find the way,
To cross the barrier where mystery lay.

Take my words and keep them near,
As in a dream to you each night I appear.
Remember me with fondness for sure;
Your love will guide me through the hardships I
endure…
(Fibby Bob Kinney (c)
He attached the poem to the pigeon's leg and it
flew off into the darkened clouds.

In the meantime…the angel soldiers had
carried Rosie back to the Moderate kingdom.
They dropped her at the bottom of the spiral
staircase that twisted its way all the way up to
her tower room. Many other angels lived on the
floors below her. It was an honor system. As
each Angel proved themselves worthy they
would occupy a room closer to the main
ballroom on the ground floor.

It was here where the chapel was located. The
angels could come here to meditate and have
their worship services. It was a beautiful
temple. Gold and jewels in all forms of art.
Wonderful paintings done by master angels.
Some with scenes showing the people of
Earth. Great sculptured statues of Angels in all

forms . Even the ceiling of the main ballroom had painted clouds and a vision of the distant kingdom of Pure Light. The far off realm where the Master and Sage Angels resided.

That was the place where the stars and the galaxies were. It was the birthplace of the supreme deities. A wonderland of mystery and consequence. All the angels of the moderate kingdom were in awe of this far off majestic kingdom.

The soldier angels dropped Rosie at the foot of the staircase. The archangel, Malickin, stood over her and said.."Go to your room. Tomorrow morning you will come here in front of the grand council. We will tell you of your punishment at that time."

With that said, he and the soldier angels left Rosie with her head bowed in anxiety.. then she drifted up the spiral staircase to her room at the top. She closed the door behind her and lay upon her bed and sobbed herself to sleep.

In the middle of the night beneath a voyeur full moon she heard a tapping on her window pane.

She looked startled and saw the pigeon fluttering its wings outside her bedroom skylight window.

She got up from the bed. Her body only clothed in a silk nightgown. The moonlight was strong and all of her youthful curves of her magnificent body were visible in the searching moonlight. She walked barefoot to the window. It was five feet above her head. She flapped her graceful wings gently and rose up to the clasp on the window. She opened it and the bird flew into her room. It landed on top of her dresser desk.

She closed the clasp on the bay window and fluttered back to the floor. She sat in her velvet clad desk chair. Her body is now warm from the exercises of her wings. She sat there in the satin silk robe now askew in her relaxed position.

The messenger bird obediently offered his foot to her. She untied the scroll and began to read Fabszy's poem in a quiet voice. The words cascading from her lips..then rebounding back up to her soft ears..

Then she took her pen and wrote this poem to him.

My dearest Fabszy,
I am sorry for what happened to you
I am sorry I was impulsive
It's my fault, had I not come to see you
Your wings wouldn't have been clipped
My grieving heart is bleeding
To think how you are suffering.
I am waiting for my punishment...
I might be thrown into the dungeon
I might be slashed a hundred times
But I willl bear the wounds and the pains
I will bear the mockery thrown at me...
Isolation, derision, ostracism,
And if ever I will be asked to forget you
I will never renounce my love for you
Even as I will face death, I will be
uttering your sweet name, Fabszy my love.

Can I not have the freedom to love
Whom my heart desires?
What is the use of love from above
If there is no pure and true love?
Why this chasm of hatred between
Our kingdoms
Labeling us as dark angels and light angels.
Does it matter to me now that you are a dark
angel ?
"I am willing to honor your name for my sake"

Your sweet angel, Rosie.
Fe Rosario V. Maximo ©

After she wrote the poem she called to the bird who sat patiently on top of her dresser desk. She attached the scroll to the leg of the pigeon. Then she talked directly to it.

" Dear courier bird. Fly swiftly to Fabszy. Give him this poem I have written to him. I have told him my feelings. Now, I want to say I care for you too. You are responsible for carrying our poems to each other. You are very important to me."

Then she took the pigeon in her hands and cuddled it to her cheek. She kissed it gently on its forehead.

The mechanical bird seemed to sense her love. The sweetness of her being. It fluttered its wings and spoke in a soft rich voice.

"Dearest Angel Rosie, I am only a mechanical bird but I have real feelings. When the angels made me they gave me a voice that I could use if I desire. This is the first time I have spoken to someone. It's just that you are so beautiful and pure that I feel special with you. You might say, in my own way I feel compassion for you. I am so happy Fabszy found you. I will talk with him when I fly back to the mountain. He doesn't know I can speak. I will tell him how much you miss him and love him dearly. I go now but I will fly back to you when Fabszy tells me how much he misses you. This way you can stay in touch with him through me.

This made Rosie happy for the first time. All she knew was misery since they snatched her away from the arms of the Angel she fell in love with. She blew a kiss to the pigeon and said, "Take my kiss with you and tell Fabszy I shall blow him a kiss every day of my life."

With that said the little mechanical pigeon furiously flapped its wings and flew out the skylight window. The moon was full and it lit up the dark sky in a golden light.

As the bird flew out the window the sentry guard in the fortress turret was waiting for him. He had seen the pigeon fly into the skylight window earlier that night and he was ready for it now that it flew into the moonlit sky. He drew back the taunt string on his bow. The arrow flew straight and true. As soon as it hit the pigeon it burst into flames. The flaming arrow and the shattered pieces of the pigeon fell to the ground below. Each piece of the bird like a tiny metal tear. They fell and took Rosie's poem and message with them, lost forever. Fabszy would never hear from this dear and faithful pigeon again. Now his and Rosie's life was in the hands of fate. Only a miracle could save them now.

Realm of Angels... Part 6
(The Punishment)

Angel Rosie had a restless sleep. She dreamt of all the incredible events that had happened to her in just the last month of her life as a nursing Angel here in the Moderate kingdom. Her life seemed to be so easy and fulfilling over her young adult years.

She had been chosen from the many to be a full nursing angel. Even though she was of virgin quality she had the gift to produce breast milk every day. Her only job was to fly to Earth and find poor unnourished children and feed them in their sleep. When the child awoke in the morning they had no recollection of Rosie's visit, only that they felt full and nourished.

This pleased Rosie very much as she adored the children. She cherished giving them the life giving milk they deserved to survive.

Now it has been two days since she visited Earth. Her breasts were swollen and filled to the brim with fresh milk. She needed to visit the children to feed them, and to relieve the pressure upon her bosom.

As she lay in bed there was a knock at her door. She got out of bed and tiptoed barefoot across the marble tile floor. She peaked out of the keyhole and saw it was Malickin the Archangel.
She immediately opened the metal and wood door to her tower bedroom.

He stood there in all his majesty. Great white wings graced his back. Strong and tall, with fiery blue eyes. The blonde hair in length covered his head as a golden crown. He was a fierce Angel and stern in his duties.

He looked down at Rosie who stood there in her sheer nightgown. Her dark hair a little disarray from the night's sleep. Still, her soft skin was flawless. Even with sleep still in her eyes she looked so beautiful. It was as if her body had an aura of pure light that hugged it and kissed her cheeks to a fine light brown texture.

She said in a quiet tone, please come in, Sir Malickin. He walked through the doorway and closed the door behind him. He looked at her sternly and said,
"You have sinned. You kissed that dark Angel and let him hold you in his arms..for that you must be punished."

Rosie blushed. "I am so sorry that happened. I take full responsibility for my actions and I will accept any punishment that you bestow upon me.
However, I do have a pressing problem. As you know I am a nursing Angel. I haven't visited Earth in two days. My breasts are swollen with fresh milk. I need to go to the children and feed them."

Malickin looked at her intently, then he spoke. " You must be punished but I will give you one small escape from your discomfort."

With that said he pushed open her silk robe and placed her breast in his mouth.

At first she was shocked then she spoke in a quivering voice.."please stop…you are hurting me..you are sucking too hard!"

In just a few seconds he drained her breast dry..he moved on to the other one. He began gulping it down

"No more, please!" She cried as the pain shot through her breast and made her upper body quiver in anxiety as he drank her sweet milk in gulps.

Then he was done. He wiped traces of the warm milk from his lips with the back of his hand and said, " I have done that small favor for you but don't expect that I will be lenient on your punishment."

Her breasts ached from the severeness of his sucking. Still, she managed a faint smile and said, thank you.

Later that morning after she had dressed and eaten a light breakfast in her room she was ready to go down to the ballroom chapel and confront the elders who would pass judgment upon her.

She looked into the mirror on her dresser table. She was radiant in the early morning sunlight. Her young face glowed as an angel in its natural beauty. Her dark hair shimmering as it flowed down to the soft, yet firmness, of her shoulders.

She wore a simple elegant looking light blue dress. It was open at a Vee at the top exposing her normally full beautiful breasts. This morning they were totally empty and flat. A testament of the harsh lips that had made them in this state of disarray.

Finally she was ready to face her peers. She glided down the long spiral staircase and entered the chapel ballroom.

All her contemporary angels were seated in rows as if at a church meeting. On the dais were the four senior angels. In the center, in the pulpit, was Malickin the Archangel. He looked directly at Rosie and said, "Let us get down to business...Rosie the nursing Angel you are charged with the crime of indecency. You have kissed a dark Angel. He has taken

you in his arms and held your body hostage
against his own.
Is all this true what I have described?

Rosie slowly bowed her head and nodded ,
"Yes".

He said, "There is further proof of your
infidelity..a while back a pigeon flew into your
bedroom window and deposited a poem upon
your bed. You were in your bathroom taking a
shower I suppose. I observed all this
happening from my perch on a hidden cloud
that overlooks your bedroom. I have been
watching you for some time now…- as I have
suspected you were up to no good.

When the pigeon left I flew into your bedroom
window and took the poem that was intended
for you ..

Then later that night as I observed, you went to
the bathroom at your regular time. I knew you
would be in there for at least ten minutes so I
snuck into your room and went through your
dresser drawer and found the poem you had
written to him..

I will read now in trial of guilt…both these poems:

Malickin opened the parchment and read the poem Fabszy had written to Rosie, aloud.

My Dearest Flower

My most dearest Rosie so sweet,
To think fondly of you is a treat.
The freshness of your endearing scent;
Upon it, my fondest emotions are spent.

So tender and loving are your arms.
They radiate beauty and charm.
The touch of your finger to my lip,
Is like heaven itself in little sips.

How I long to hold you in surprise;
Touching you completely until sunrise.
The undulating folds of your hair,
Entices my eyes to continually stare.

To touch your bare toes with my own.
Togetherness is our very home.
Come to me now in your dream;
I worship you as being supreme..
(Fibby Bob Kinney (c)

After he finished reading Fabszy's poem there
was a look of disgust on his face.
He cringed, looked directly at Rosie and
said…"and this is the poem that I found that
you wrote to him"

Malickin stood straight up in the pulpit
and with a stern look on his face began to read
the poem Rosie had written to Fabszy…

Parting Days

My days when we are apart
Are likened to a parched land
Suffering from drought.
We must no longer be alone and apart
That would leave us empty and forlorn
Take care of yourself, my dearest love
Everytime I think that you may be sick
I die and cry , not being able to nurse you
and bring you back your strength.
If ever loneliness comes over you
When days are gloomy and chilly
Imagine my arms keeping you warm.

Can there be more precious than our love
I will give up everything for you.
For what good is life without you?
Keep yourself strong for me

Never succumb to despair
I will appeal to the deities
To look on you with mercy
That you will be delivered
From your horrendous state.

I hope our sufferings will pass
We shall overcome all obstacles
Our love is stronger than a bedrock
Our love is formidable
Nothing can destroy it.
Deep in my heart i know our love
is never lost
Love endures ; it will survive.
Like a sturdy tree that grows taller
Yet its roots grow deeper
Storms can not throw it down.

Let us not be faint and give up
We will survive, remember dearest
My desire for you can not be quenched
Until we are together again
"Amor fati ", I must love to fulfill my fate.
(Fe Rosario V. Maximo (c)

After Malickin read the poem he threw it to the
chapel floor. He looked directly at Rosie and
said, "The poem you wrote to that dark Angel
disgusts me. How dare you speak with a

passion in your voice to that filthy angel who has carnal wishes!"

Rosie looked up intently and said, " He is not a filthy Angel. There was an admiration in his eyes when he looked at me. There were times when I walked down the long hall on my way to nurse the children and I saw you looking at me. I saw an admiration in your eyes too. "

Malickin's wings shot up. He yelled in a loud voice. " How dare you talk to me like that. Are you saying you saw lust in my eyes for you?"

Rosie looked at him gently and said, "No Sir, I said there was admiration in your eyes."

Malickin was now fuming. " Don't you turn your words around you hussy wicked Angel. You insinuate that I had a lustful stare at you. That I wanted to ravish you. How dare you think that of me. I shall make your punishment severe so you will know no-one can question the motives of an archangel.
Starting immediately your nursing privileges are revoked."

Rosie in a desperate attempt to make sense of all of this suddenly blurted out.."You can't do that sir. I carry fresh milk in my breasts every day. I must feed it to the hungry children."

Malickin sneered. Your nursing privileges are over. Each morning you will dump your breast milk down the sink. You are a tarnished Angel.
In addition to that -each day after lunch and dinner you will clear up all the dirty dishes and wash them by yourself. Then you will clean the public bathrooms in the entire tower kingdom. You are banned from ever visiting Earth again.
Now go, your duties will begin tomorrow morning. As for today, I want you to get down on your hands and knees and wash the floor of your bedroom and bathroom. This will get you in touch with what your punishment is each day from now till the years end. I have spoken, so let it be."

There was a hush in the entire chapel hall. All the other angels were horrified by the severeness of the punishment. They never made a murmur as they knew how strong the discipline from Malickin the archangel could be.

Rosie, still with her head bowed, glided up the long staircase to her bedroom.
As soon as she got inside and closed the iron and oak door..she fell to her knees. She wept,

as precious water cascaded from her eyes. Then, she scrubbed the marble floor with her own tears.

Realm of Angels … Part 7
(The Sacrifice)

Angel Rosie lay upon her bed in the turret room of the kingdom of the moderate angels. She was devastated. There was no hope for her now. Her punishment was so severe.

"How could he do this to me?" She murmured to herself. He is an archangel of such immense power. Why is there no forgiveness in his heart? Yes, I did kiss and fall in love with a dark Angel. Still, both our intentions were pure. It is a genuine love we share for each other. Yet, Sir Malickin will not forgive me, even a little. Even after he hurt me so much when he sucked the breast milk from me, the life giving milk I am required to deliver to the poor starving children on Earth. He took that honorable privilege from me….now I must empty my breast milk in the sink. Only to helplessly watch it go down the drain. How cruel a punishment, along with washing floors and cleaning the public bathrooms every day for the entire next year.

Rosie buried her head in the soft goose down pillow and cried openly as she pondered her tortured reality. Then she looked up and saw some tiny shards of metal glowing on the window sill of the bay window at the top of her room.

She fluttered her wings and flew up to the window. When she opened it the metal pieces fell into her hand. They were part of the wings of the mechanical pigeon.

She flopped to her bed in horror. She realized the magic pigeon that had been the courier between her and the dark Angel Fabszy was dead. It must have been shot down by the sentry guard as it flew from her window carrying her poem to Fabszy.

She nearly screamed when she thought of that hot arrow hitting the pigeon and making it explode. Now there was no way to contact Fabszy and tell him of her longing for his safety and well being.

She made the decision right then and there. She would give up her rights as a moderate Angel and fly to the mountain where Fabszy was a prisoner. His wings were useless and he was lost in that huge forest.

Without another thought to stop her she gathered together her personal possessions. She left a note on her bed addressed to the Archangel Malickin. It read Sir Malickin you have deserted all the good in me. I will never return to this kingdom again. I forgive you for the harsh punishments you have put upon me. Please be more lenient in your thoughts when you deal with the other angels who only want to do good deeds with their powers. I will miss the children and hope they will survive without me as their nursing angel..
As my breast milk is now useless to them."

She folded the parchment and put it on top of her bed. Then, with a small satchel in her hand she flew out of the skylight window into the darkening night sky.

The sentry guard who was usually diligent was now in a light sleep. He had killed the courier pigeon and he thought all would be safe now. So he dozed off in a snoring sleep. He never saw Rosie fly out of her bedroom window and disappear into the graying night sky.

Rosie glided through the clouds. She was not sure where she was going. The big glowing moon sensed her need. It shone its moonlit rays through the darkened clouds. Rosie followed their lead and the moonbeams led her to the forest at the secret mountain.

She flew down through the clouds and landed in a clearing near the trees. At first, all she saw was a forest full of magnificent trees and flowers.

To get a better look she flew up from the ground and tried to fly into the forest. She was stopped cold and bounced off of the protective shield that surrounded the forest. She tried to fly over it but that was impossible. The shield covered the entire huge forest in a protective dome. There was no way to penetrate it. There was no way to see beyond the treetops..as the interior of the forest was masked in a golden haze.

Angel Rosie then spied a wishing well at the outside perimeter of the forest. She glided to it and landed next to the well.

She was amazed by its beautiful structure. She went up to the Crystal bucket and cranked it down into the wishing well. When she brought it back up it was full of fresh clear water. Then she drank her fill of this precious tasting, life giving, healing water.

It made her feel as a whole being. She was full of excitement. After she drank, she thought, "There must be a door to get into that forest and she would find it."

Then, her enthusiasm came to an abrupt end. She looked around the well and for the first time she noticed the human bones. Upon closer look she realized these were the skeletons of travelers who had come here and couldn't find the opening to the forest's interior entrance.

She began to cry, "Do some of these bones belong to the Angel Fabszy ? This thought nearly crippled her mind.

Her tears rolled down her cheeks and mingled with the well water in the crystal bucket she held in her trembling hands. She laid the bucket back to the well and sat beside it.

She reached inside her travel bag and took out her quill pen and parchment paper. She said to herself.."I shall write this poem in lament to Fabszy. I fear he is gone forever. I will write this poem to his memory and then I will throw myself down that deep well. I will join him in paradise."

With that said, she took the pen in her Angel's beautiful hand and wrote this poem;

My dear Fabszy,
wherever you are I hope you can hear me.
I am all alone grieving over your demise
I never thought I would ever see you again.
I had high hopes that we would live a new life
Live in a world away from peering eyes.
A world we build is founded on love and peace.
So far from a world of hatred and animosity
I dreamt of a paradise of serenity
A beautiful world where we can move freely
 Where we can raise our own lovely family
Watch our brilliant children grow lovingly
Fly in the sky , dancing gracefully and gayly.

And when the day is done
We will retire in our love sanctuary
You will tenderly take me into your arms
I will kiss away your worries and concerns

I will read you poetry, sing you a lullaby
Till you fall asleep , and the cares vanish away.

With your passing all dreams have died.
Days without you are bleak and dark.
The songbirds sing nothing but dirges
The sun won't shine , only an avalanche
Of cold searing pains and sorrows
Why has Fate been cruel to us?
Our love was pure and true.
Why would you be taken away from me?
You are my happiness, my reality
No one can doubt our love's purity.
What will happen to me?
Living alone, no one to protect me.
No shoulders to lean on
No chest to rest upon
No kisses to wipe away my tears.

Oh, I speak to the sky above!
How miserable I am? Life is meaningless!
I can no longer bear this gnawing loneliness
I feel I have been thrown into a dark abyss
There seems no escape from ferocious lions
Eagerly waiting to tear my body into pieces
No one to rescue me from the hungry mouths
of beasts.
The nightingale has stopped singing happily

There's no one to console me, I am all alone in
misery.

I have hugged your dry bones
I kissed them, breathed on them
Shed my tears on them,
Hoping a divine miracle will happen
And you will be back to life.
But all is in vain.
Darling come to me even in my dreams
I desperately need your presence
Cold are my nights and days
Touch me. Let me feel your warmth
Or I'll die!
Angel Rosie.
(Fe Rosario Vergara- Maximo (c)

After she finished the poem she placed it on
top of the canopy that covered the well. Then
she noticed the black backpack laying near the
bushes. She remembered when the soldier
angels carried her off Malarkin, the Archangel
was so busy yelling slurs at Fabszy he forgot
the backpack with the shears in it as he flew off
into the dark sky.

She walked over and picked up the pack. Upon
opening it she saw the flaming shears still

inside. With her hands shaking she pulled the shears from the pack and said…

"This beast stole the wings from my dearest Fabszy. He had to walk the Earth with the power in his wings gone forever. I will clip my own wing tips off. This way I can feel the pain and misery he must have felt before his demise."

With that said, she took the flaming scissor blades and cut off the precious wing tips that granted her flight. She fell to the ground sobbing. Her wings now as useless baggage upon her back.

As soon as she had cut off her wing tips the poem shc had written began to glow. It began to shimmer upon the glass canopy above the wishing well. The wingtips of the lamenting Angel had flown to it. The moment Rosie cut her wings a higher power inhabited them and brought them to her poem. Now it had wings and it began to fly.

The poem flew past a group of trees still outside the doom but hidden from view. Fabszy lay there, totally exhausted, and near the throws of death's grip. He lay at the foot of the magic doorway that led into the forest kingdom.

As he lay there his fingers touched the magic door. He had tried so hard but there was no way to pass its mysterious message.

He took his plumed pen and wrote this poem as a farewell:

Goodbye to Happiness

My dearest Rosie of lost love,
I go now to peace in the sky above.
No longer to flap my wings,
Life for me will no longer sing.

I'm a goner without a home.
Destined for my spirit to roam.
If only I could see your smile once more;
To tell you how completely your Angel eyes I adore.

To try one's best is a trait of honor;
To look past what made one a goner.
All I remember is my love for you.
It is in my heart steadfast and true.

Take these last words you may never hear,

Know that with my last breath I draw you near.
Hear me in your heart of gold;
The time we spent together will never grow old.
(Fibby Bob Kinney (c)

Fabszy clutched the poem in his hands. The wingtips the Archangel had cut off suddenly came alive. They attached themselves to the parchment paper of Fabszy's poem and it flew out of his clenched fingers. They flew the poem back to Rosie.

She was standing on the rim of the wishing well. Ready to throw herself down the long shaft to drown in the well's deep water. She wanted to be with Fabszy even if it was meant to be pure nothingness..they would still be together forever.

As she was ready to make the leap into oblivion…Fabszy's feather driven poem landed on her finger tips. She read it intently.

After she finished she realized he must still be alive. With the poem in her hand she followed it closely behind. Her dead wings were a burden upon her back. She struggled to keep up with the flying poem.

And then she saw him. Laying there, in a state of being near death, at the foot of the magic doorway to the hidden kingdom…He was clutching the poem she had written to him in his hands.

She approached him, knelt down, and cuddled him in her arms. She said with a tremble in her voice.

"I am no longer an Angel, as I have cut off my wingtips. I still have the breast milk in me from my duty as a nursing angel. My breasts are full one last time. I shall give you the milk so you may live and be strong again.

With that said, she slipped her warm breast out of her blouse and placed it in Fabszy's mouth. He immediately began to suckle upon it.

Rosie bent her head down to Fabszy's ear and whispered softly, " please don't suck so hard."

Fabszy immediately stopped sucking. He looked up and said, " I am so sorry, I never want to hurt you, please forgive me."

Rosie smiled, "your touch will never hurt me. I am yours. To please you with all that I do..with all that you need from me, is my desire to give to you."

Fabszy leaned deeper into her bosom. He kissed her breast gently and began nursing as if a little baby in all its purity to fill its hunger in life.

After Fabszy had his fill. He felt strong and virile again. He reached up and kissed Rosie on her lips. She could taste the warmness of the milk on his lips. She was proud that her nursing duties could end in this way of giving life to her loved one.
After the kiss they arose to their feet.
The magic doorway was glowing. The Puzzle message engraved upon the shimmering oak and golden door, began to speak..you have solved the riddle of the words; "Let All Ye who wish to enter find the True and Only Way"

It is the love within one's heart for the welfare of another that is the secret of passage. You have shown that you both would have given your life to protect one another. Pass through the portal now..and find your happiness."

With that said..the flaming doorway opened and Fabszy and Rosie stepped into a new wonderland of mystery and adventure.

Realm of Angels: Part 8
(The New Kingdom)

Fabszy and Rosie stood there hand in hand. The portal gate had opened. The flaming words above the rim burned brightly…"Let all Ye who wish to enter- find the True and Only Way"..they had conquered this puzzle with the undying pledge of love together.
They were ready for anything. All that mattered was to be with each other.
Nothing could separate them now. They had been through too much, had passed many tests, and found that their love had conquered the obstacles that tried to drive them apart.

It was a match of two opposite forces: he, a daring Angel of the deep desires…she, an

Angel of the equalizer of moderate desires.
Together they had found a union where they
emerged in a balance of longing and innocent
feelings combined…it was a feeling of
happiness and joy to explore the properties of
love.
****

Meanwhile,in another part of the Magic Forest
a different story was taking place…

He had chiseled these words upon a marble
tombstone.

"A grace not yet filled.
My knightly deeds not yet done,
As there were more battles to be won.
Still, my grave awaits;
Its glory beneath heaven's gates.
A tribute to a gentle, yet fierce soul,
As upon my own deeds I did enroll."

High in the clouds a falcon watched the ancient
knight intently. The falcon was a magic
priestess who had followed this knight's
illustrious career. She had seen him as
champion of the Old Kingdom; the castle ruled
by the knight monks.

They worshiped Nature. Their oath was to protect the forest and its animals. The great forest had been here since the early days of the first century when humans took power.

Before them, the animals had roamed in savagery. Huge beasts commanded the forest. They devoured the smaller animals. All were in fear of these colossal giants. Then, the human animal was born. They were as ferocious as the bigger beasts and they realized that they were smarter than the wild beasts that had dominated for so long.

This new species of animal evolved into the rulers of the forest. The big animals were no match for them anymore. These new Men and Women, as they called themselves, were smart and cunning.

They built castles and beautiful gardens. They learned art and music. Now, the only real enemy they had were each other…as with knowledge came the need for power.

Kingdoms sprang up in the four quadrants of the great forest. Each with their own king as ruler. The four kings constantly tried to outdo each other. Hence, there were many battles fought for pride…and to covet the spoils of battle.

Each kingdom had their quota of knights. The trained warriors of battle.
They lived separate from the castle. As each kingdom had a monastery where the knights resided. They trained hard and prayed to Nature. They believed in magic. There were mages and warlords that were the mystic guides in each kingdom.

From the women in each kingdom the most beautiful and talented were trained as high priestesses. They were taught magic formulas. The highest of this rank had a connection with divine entities that ruled the sky above.

One of the most formidable of these high priestesses was from the kingdom of the East. Her name is "Anneto- the guardian falcon". She is a beautiful young woman with the power to transform herself into a peregrine falcon. She could fly high and penetrate the clouds with her keen eyesight. Nothing escaped her gaze. For the past 20 years she had been observing one particular knight from the kingdom of the West. The direct rival of the kingdom of the East.

These two kingdoms were constantly in conflict. As were the kingdoms of the North and South: continuous battles were fought in the name of justice and liberty.
Although there was no clear winner…as all four kingdoms had knights of equal strength and valor.

This knight that the priestess Anneto had been watching all these years was named Fabbo. He was particularly agile and ferocious in battle. She had seen him slay as many as fifty foes in one battle. An extraordinary number even for the champion knight.

What she saw beside his fearless nature was a gentle way about him. He seemed to be friendly with the small animals of the forest. When he was near they came to him. They playfully licked his sandals and cuddled next to him.

This intrigued Anneto. She followed his exploits intently. He had aged past the point where he had the strength of his youth. He carried many scars of battle. Now he was retired at the knights monastery. His job was to chop wood

for the many fireplaces that kept the rooms
warm in the cool air of the East.

Today was different from the other days.
At first all she saw was the large marble
tombstone. Then through her falcon eyes she
saw the words he had chiseled upon it.
She, from a great distance, bore down on the
message he wrote.

"I chisel my words upon a tombstone.
A grace not yet filled.
My knightly deeds not yet done,
As there are more battles to be won.
Still, my grave awaits;
Its glory beneath heaven's gates.
A tribute to a gentle, yet fierce soul,
As upon my own deeds I did enroll…

After she had read these words, again,
with powerful strokes she flew high into the
upper clouds. A flock of screaming geese
cheered her on..wishing for one tenth of her
flying power. She circled the sky, ever watching
the knight. She could see the sweat on his
brow..as this falcon was a superior winged
mystic of the skies. It was her heritage, as she
was born of the wind on that day of discovery

of her true self. "Anneto" champion of the Krown Clan.

She remembered his last testament that he chiseled into the smooth stone. Then, she realized these were his last words.
She thought only for a moment. Then she folded her falcon wings into a steep dive.

She flew to the ground where the knight stood. He was bare to the waist. His chest and back are covered with scars. Some from whips that cracked upon him while in dungeon chains. His body was still somewhat strong but the years of battle had worn him down. He was old by knight standards, but still, he had his valor under control.

As soon as the falcon landed on the wood pile that he had made from his chopping all morning long. She spoke in a clear female voice.

"I know who you are, valiant knight. You are Fabbo, the fallen champion of the Old Realm."

Fabbo was astonished. He quickly put on his leather vest to cover the scars on his upper body. Embarrassing he said quietly,

"Forgive me, Magic Falcon. I have heard of your powers. This is my first sighting of you."

The falcon fluttered her wings and flew directly to Fabbo's face.

He looked astonished as the falcon with her wingtips fluttering opened Fabbo's mouth and blew her breath upon his lips.

An amazing transformation took place. His scars disappeared and his body gained the strength of his youth.

He stood tall and strong. Then, he reached for his ancient battered sword. A thousand notches on its blade. Onc for each enemy that felt its final bite.

He looked at the falcon and said.."I am honored that you gave me back my strength as my enemies will feel the taste of my blade before nightfall"

The falcon replied ..I have given you youth but it is only for one day. Even my best magical powers cannot extend its reach beyond tomorrow."

The knight bowed and said, "One day is all I need. My enemies shall fall before me and in the end I shall fall on my sword..in glory." With that said. His Helmet and Shield at the ready. He marched into the valley of doom..to fulfill his vow..

The falcon flew high into the sky..to watch from her perch on the highest cloud.

Then she said to herself.."I wonder if I should have told him;
When he falls on his sword..he will become an Angel- just like me…fBk

Realm of Angels…part 9.
(An Eagle is Born)

Fabbo, now restored to his young knightley body, was steaming. The air was cool and even frosty on a damp Autumn day. Yet, it felt like a surge to his perspiring body. His aged muscles had grown taunt and strong. He could feel the vigor of youth surging through his veins. The armor of his days as champion of the Old Realm still fit him perfectly.

Ah, his sword. The iron forged blade. Strong as steel in its master forging. A thousand foes had felt the bite of his blade. Now a hundred more must fall before this day is done. How was it possible to slay 100 barbarians in one battle? The most foes he slain were 55. He remembered after that siege he was exhausted even after a full day of rest.

It didn't matter. Mosswag…leader of the Fungg..he had personally killed Fabbo's horse and his fighting pet, the Wolfhound. He cut them down with that huge double edge axe..the one that supposedly slew a legion of knights, by his hand alone. Yes, he was formidable, still, his weakness was in his left elbow. A centaur had kicked him there and broken the bone before Mosswag had slain him.

Fabbo thought to himself…"when I get to him in the battle..his left arm will be my prize ".

And now he was ready. His armor and shield were almost impregnable. His sword and dagger the very best. His throwing knives loaded in a belt around his waist. And his sling with the stone marbles. He could twirl it so fast that the marble would penetrate even solid armor to find his mark. Now loaded for battle he took his most trusted weapon..the longbow, with flaming tip arrows. They burst into flames as soon as they hit their target. Then they exploded and at times took out two or more foes at once. He made sure the explosive power was fresh on each arrow.

Finally, he was ready. His horse and dog were gone…still he had the bull that the monastery kept to keep the cows happy.
It was a massive creature, with horns so pointy and sharp. They could penetrate even iron plate…and today they would be put to the test.

Fabbo was the only knight the bull would let get near him. He felt a kinship for Fabbo.
Today he sensed he would give his life to protect this valiant knight of the Old Kingdom.

Fabbo mounted the bull. Its hoof's digging clumps of dirt. Its nostrils flaring smoke and fire as it charged headlong into the barbaric encampment.

They were unprepared. Drunk and dizzy from a continuous party of savagery. Goblets of wine, some half spilled, others frothing with foam.

Savage warriors, half naked. Dancing girls in a crazed dance with bare breasts bobbing. Jugglers and jesters laughing and calling each other obscene names.
It was a pagan ritual gone to a state of wickedness and excess.

Fabbo on the Bull charged headlong into the midst of the Frey. Bodies were flying everywhere. The bull with its horns like a rapier cut through the drunken barbarian soldiers like a windmill. Their naked bodies flying through the air like confetti at a party.

Fabbo jumped off the bull. With his bow spouting flaming arrows..the foes fell in heaps. His arrows spent …he drew his sword.

A large number of barbarians came to their senses and grabbed their clubs and axes and charged Fabbo.

The faithful Bull threw himself in front of Fabbo and took the brunt of the charge. They clubbed him fiercely until the Bull finally gave a mournful sound and crashed to the sawdust strewn floor. It lay there quiet and serene in its passing.

This so infuriated Fabbo. This magnificent bull had given his life for him. With a terrible scream he charged the gang of ruffians who stood before him.

With his iron sword in his powerful grip he slew every man in sight. Suddenly he looked around and there was not a sound to be heard. Only moans from the few foes still with breath as the entire grand dining chamber was destroyed. A hundred vicious foes lay dead on this massive floor.

Fabbo stood there, his body aching and shaking. He had taken a few hits and blood was oozing from his wounds. Still he felt strong and able.

Then he heard a billowing voice at the far end of the Great hall…"Fabbo, I am impressed. You have managed to wipe out my entire army. A feat I would have thought impossible. Yet, you managed to do a miracle. Still, I see you are wounded..blood runs from your side and shoulders. I will finish you off quickly…then he added , "So you won't have to suffer like your horse and dog..before I slew them!"

When Fabbo heard these words it triggered a storm within him. His heart began to beat like a jungle drum. Calling the warrior within him to peak battle form...once again.

In a fluid motion he took the sling from the pouch around his neck. He loaded a large marble stone in it. Then in a swift motion he raised his hand ..he twirled the sling at an impossible twirling speed. When he let it go the marble granite stone was flying at near the speed of sound...it hit Mosswag directly on the left elbow...shattering it. The barbaric king fell to the floor screaming in pain.

Fabbo was on him in an instant. He looked down at Mosswag and said..I shall slay you with your own axe."

He reached down and snatched the axe from the king's fingers..he raised the double edged axe over his head.. then, gripping it with both hands, he said.." This is payment for my horse and dog... The axe crashed down upon Mosswag's chest, nearly cutting him in half.

Still at the last moment the barbaric king managed to reach up and grab Fabbo's sword. He plunged it into Fabbo's ribs.

As soon as Fabbo had slain the king. He realized the prophecy came true. He teetered for a moment and fell directly on his sword.

He lay there dying. Anneto, in the form of the falcon flew to his side. She spoke in a quiet tone…" I saw the whole battle. You were magnificent. Now you are near death".

She took a crystal bottle that was hidden beneath her wing. She spoke again softly. "I shall breathe my breath into this bottle."..

She popped off the cork and blew a breathy kiss into the bottle."
Then spoke in a whisper.

"When you die I shall capture your last breath and it will be in this bottle to mingle with my own….
Then, when our breath is mixed together…I will place it beneath your nose..when you sniff it in …you will be reborn again."

As soon as he heard her words he took his last breath. With her wingtip feathers she quickly uncorked the bottle, placed it under his nose, and captured his last breath…

She twirled the bottle and her breath mingled with his then she placed the bottle back under his nose. He took one sniff and as the Phoenix.. he rose up from his ashes and came alive.

At first he was astonished. Then he realized he wasn't a man anymore. His being had been replaced by a bird. He was now a full grown Eagle.

Anneto looked longing at him and said. "I know, it's hard to imagine but you are now a bird….I had to pay a steep price to bring you back to life.
The elders of my tribe demanded that I forfeit my body as a woman..then you may live. They granted me one wish.. I chose that you become a bird like me..instead of a Man. Please forgive me for this choice. I did all this because I love you. If you choose..the other choice you have is I can die now and you will be born as a man again."

Fabbo, as the Eagle, his great wing's a flutter, bowed before Anneto. He spoke solemnly,

"My dearest Anneto you have saved me. I am an Eagle..a knight of the sky. I want to spend the rest of my life with you."

With that said he drew closer and embraced her in his wings. At that moment they felt the deepest love possible for each other.

Anneto the falcon, her head resting upon Fabbo's feathery chest said in a whimsical tone.

"My parents, the King and Queen, of the Krown Clan.. will be shocked when I tell them I am going to marry an Eagle!"

Then she quickly looked up and said.."You do mean to marry me..don't you?"

The great Eagle,his eyes ablaze with love, replied...."You will be my bride. I shall never leave your side.we are birds..the winged angels of the Great Forest!"

Anneto flapped her wings in joy.."Wow, are Mom and Dad in for a surprise!'

Realm of Angels...Part 10
(The Royal Wedding)

Anneto and Fabbo flew deep into the clouds. She was fast and agile. Fabbo was just getting used to his new wings. This was his first flight..and he was learning fast. Together they played hide and seek in the massive cloud cover. At first she had him stumped. He just couldn't keep up with her. So quick, as a falcon, she took to the skies with ease. Soon, though, he began to master the art of flying. His Eagle wings were huge. He learned how to dip and dive and make sharp turns. They played in the clouds all day long.

It was nearing nightfall. Anneto gilded her way to the walls of the Krown Clan Castle. It was a magnificent structure. Great stone walls surrounded this fortress. The guards posted at the century points recognized her immediately and let her and her companion pass the outer wall easily. The Castle Krown was an impregnable fortress. It was built from solid stone blocks. The turrets were Iron reinforced. Still, the gardens inside the walls were magnificent. Lush flowers grew everywhere. Trees of all types swayed on the hallowed ground of this great structure.

Anneto and Fabbo landed just outside the main dining hall. The King and Queen were having dinner with invited guests. Queen Tiva saw her daughter first and stood to greet her.

"There you are my darling! We missed you so much. You are just in time for dinner. I see you brought a guest. Some kind of magic prince I suppose. Ok, quickly change your shape from that falcon to your human form.. and tell your guest to do the same!"

With that said, she turned to her husband the king and said, "Saygar, your daughter and her friend are joining us for dinner."

She turned back to face her daughter and said, "Why haven't you changed to your human form yet?"

Anneto spoke in a troubled voice. "That is a big problem I have to tell you and dad about. I have given up my right to be human to save this knight from being killed. The elders gave me no choice…his life for my privilege forfeited to be human. Now, as he, I must be a bird for the rest of my life."

Queen Tiva gasped. She blurted out…"I can't believe my ears. You gave up your right to be human..to be a bird?…Why?"

Anneto just shrugged her wings and said…"Because I love Fabbo..I want to spend the rest of my life as his bride… we are going to be married."

When King Saygar heard those words he choked on a leg of pheasant that he was eating ….He nearly screamed
"My daughter wants to marry a bird?"

Anneto quickly corrected him…"He's not just a bird.. He is an Eagle…and a really fast one too!"

The King wiped his mouth and said, "Oh, that is supposed to make a difference!..I lost a daughter and gained a bird, excuse me, and Eagle as a son!"

The Queen spoke …"Yes, it's true my dear. But she said she loves him.. and that is what really matters."

The King caved in…"He looked at Fabbo and said …"I haven't even heard you speak yet, still, If Anneto says she loves you ..and you love her ..then I shall not prevent you from your happiness."

Fabbo spoke for the first time. " My King and Queen.. Your daughter has saved my life. I was a knight of the Old Kingdom and she gave me the strength to slay my enemies…and I love her with all my heart."

The King interrupted, "You are Fabbo the Knight…I have heard of your prowess in battle.. you are the slayer of fifty men at the siege of the West Castle. That is a remarkable feat of chivalry

Anneto spoke up…"Well daddy, if you think that was something… he slew the whole barbarian band of ruffians before he died.. and I resurrected him. I want to be his bride..for all of my life."

Both parents looked at each other and nodded. The King said in his authoritative tone…"Then so shall it be..We will give you a royal wedding tomorrow."

Anneto flew to her father and embraced him with her wings. Fabbo stood in front of the

Queen and bowed to her majestically. The next day the wedding was to be.

The two birds slept peacefully that night. In the morning with the first rays of the Sun.., the Castle was in a flurry of preparation. The great banquet hall was transformed into a wedding chapel. Flowers everywhere, beautiful decorations filled the massive hall to make it look like a royal wedding was to take place.

And by noon that day. That is exactly what happened. The bride was dressed in white. Actually she had her hairdresser touch up her feather in a white non toxic paint. As a falcon who wears a hood.,she had a veil over her head. She sat upon the glove of her father's hand as he called her down the aisle to the marriage ritual.

Fabbo looked magnificent as he stood with the preacher as he watched his bride coming down the aisle. There were many guests in the gathering. Some Royalty from the East Kingdom. The royal guard of knights were there.
Some of them snickering under their breath ...."Can you believe that bird used to be a knight?

Others chuckled, "Knightley Bird…One swoop
of my sword and he is done!!"
Others giggled with him.

Even as Anneto in her regal beauty came
down the aisle…there were women in the
crowd who were talking softly to each other.

"She is marrying an Eagle, isn't that a mixed
marriage?'
Another replied, "Yea, she was foolish enough
to be a bird…but she couldn't pick someone
from her own species.. like another falcon guy
wasn't good enough for her?

Among the good well wishers there was always
some who think that if things are a little
different..they are wrong.It's hard to be free
from prejudice if things aren't the way they are
supposed to be .

Fabbo and Anneto were married that day. They
were very happy and in love. Still they had to
pay the price for being different.

Their love was so strong that nothing seemed
to matter to them. As happiness was in their
eyes..and wings of flight.

Realm of Angels.......part 11
(The Honeymoon)

Overall the wedding was a great success.
Fabbo and Anneto were now wed together. It
mattered not their differences. He, a Golden
Eagle; one of the fastest, largest raptors. Gold
feathers gleaned brown as he was a knight of
the sky. She, a peregrine Falcon with
unbelievable speed and agility. Together, they
were the Royalty and commanders of the
clouds.

Yes, beneath their outer appearance they were
true angels. Their wings in plain sight to the
testimony of their heritage. These two birds of
different breeds were madly in love with each
other. Now,it was time to mate together. So
wonderful and spiritual…as both were virgins
to this ritual.

They flew and played the rest of the day up
high in the clouds. Dashing in and out of the
fluffy, pillowed whiteness of the heavens
above. As powerful and swift was he, with the
great wingspan to cover the sky like a streak of
lightning with wings. Still, with all of his great
maneuvers she still could out dive him. No bird

in the sky had the aerodynamics of the Falcon in a steep dive. She could reach breakneck speed and at the last moment swoop up out of the dive to float effortlessly in the still cool air. So breathtaking to watch. The animals on the ground would look up and see these acrobats put on a show.

Finally, the great Sun that had been obversiving all from its roost in the distant sky..began to dip its huge head over the horizon.

The two birds, exhausted now, looked down for a place to land. There it was, as if appearing out of a storybook, "The Honeymoon Inn". A sanctuary for travelers, both human and animal. This was an all species welcome resort.

They landed in unison right at the front desk. The clerk, an older Elf. He had been in the employ of the Inn for many years, and had seen it all. So, when two birds approached him for a room, he was not surprised.

As they approached the front desk he spoke first ...."Well, if it isn't the royal couple...I heard about the wedding. Two of my elf buddies work as gardeners in the floral hothouse. They told me all about your wedding..Elpie, made the corsage the Queen was wearing!"

Anneto perked up..."Yes, I remember seeing that, and the bouquets the bridesmaid Robins were carrying in their beaks."

"Yes, that was Elpie's creation, too. Ok, let's get down to business. I have the Bridal Suite reserved for you. It's that big cage penthouse up on the roof of this building. One of our finest accommodations. We do get a number of royal birds here from time to time.. they prefer that old time birdcage look. It's a feeling that unites humans and birds in one environment.

Fabbo spoke up...."Sounds like a plan. We will take it. "

Elpie grinned..."this is the key to the room. We don't want any flying geese to try to sneak in ...if you know what I mean!"

They all gave a whistle which is kind of a bird laugh. Fibbo took the key in his talon and he and Anneto flew up to the penthouse birdcage.

As soon as they entered Fibbo locked the cage room door. Anneto drew the massive blinds to close the view of the night sky. A million stars and twinkled down at them. The blinds were closed but still the full moon found a way to light the room in a golden light. There was a big round bed in the center of the room. Anneto flopped herself upon it. She gave a birdie giggle, "This is great!..come on…big guy of the sky..give it a try!"

Fabbo flew beside her in the bed. They looked into each other's eyes. His great golden wings folded around her. It was both an amorous and a protective gesture. He said softly into her ear.."You are so beautiful, so perfect, I love you with all the joy in my heart."

Anneto blushed, then she said, "this will be our first time to experience the mating ritual. I have waited all my life for this moment. Everything I have will be yours tonight. There is nothing I will keep from you.. no need to ask, take what you will of me…as all of my being is yours…please take me into your heart and let me feel it's beating upon my breast."

Fibbo felt the urge beyond his wish for desire.. he was experiencing true love with his bride…His wings shivered with a feeling of joy…"Yes, oh Yes,my darling Anneto …I am yours for the asking, for the taking of my love, I am yours.."

They mated together with the voyeur moon as their witness, and a million stars in the sky to cheer them into total happiness.

Afterwards they enjoyed the rainwater shower that was at the far end of the room. They bathed together and forgot all their cares and worries as they kissed and caressed each other.

They lay back on the bed. Anneto said with a smile on her face…she said with a little grin in her voice…"When I first met you..as a human, you were writing a poem on that tombstone. Well, actually, you were chiseling it into the solid marble stone. It will remain there for many lifetimes.. maybe forever. You are a wonderful poet.. can you write a poem for me …now!"

Fabbo thought for a moment then he replied, "Yes, I remember that. The ability to write has always come naturally to me. I still have my human wits about me. Yes, I will make a poem just for you."

He fluttered to the desk at the other side of the room. There was paper and a bottle of ink there. He took them and with the talon of his right foot he dipped it into the ink.

He gave a little laugh and said, "They know that birds don't need a pen..they write with the talons of their feet."   With that said, he began his poem to his bride

The Closeness of Love

What is this feeling never felt before;
To touch someone to adore.
A meeting with a body brand new;
An intoxicating virgin brew.

To plow a new field where love is born;
Upon one's honor to hold and adorn,
The sweetness of the cherry tree,
Beneath its branches to covet thee.

Take my honor in one's grasp.
To give it up freely, at last.
Two virgin flowers in the rain;
Our tears together are the gain.

Hold me in your sacred arms tight.
I give you everything I am tonight.
Let the Moon know our love is true.
For, tonight, it began from brand new.
Fibby Bob Kinney ©

Fibbo took the poem and placed it upon Anneto's heaving chest. Then he lay upon her, again. The poem upon the paper flapped in unison to the beating, the thrashing of their wings…as they sang themselves into ecstasy!

Realm of Angels…part 12
(Fabbo's Freedom)

Fabbo watched Anneto fly out of their bridal suite at the "The Honeymoon Inn" which was at the beginning of the Great Forest. The two virgin birds had not yet consummated their marriage vows. Then, that pigeon arrived with a letter from Anneto's parents. The King and Queen of The East Kingdom. "Was this all a dream?" Fabbo kept saying to himself. They were laying there in the honeymoon bed, entwined in each other's wings and suddenly that pigeon appeared. "Was this some kind of an omen? Is a family member sick? Perhaps a war was declared with the rival West Kingdom?....all these thoughts raced through Fabbo's eagle brain. He lay back on the bed and tried to rest until he heard more from Anneto... She promised she would get word to him as soon as she found out what the mystery was in her parents kingdom.

Anneto with her falcon wings in a dashing furry flew through the dark sky. It was nearing morning and the Sun was starting to rise in the east. She could see past the valleys and trees to the clearing where the Castle of the East lay. Torch light was visible on the turrets and castle walls. As she flew closer she could see the sentries, some with their bows with flaming arrows drawn to the hilt. The Captain of the guard recognized her as she approached. His men immediately put down their bows and he bid her safe passage over the walls. She flew directly to the Royal Library. The Stained Glass picture window was open. It showed a collage of a band of heavenly angels singing to a young princess dancing around a marble fountain... as she flew in through that window she made a note in her mind that she was the subject of that painting mosaic. For a second, she remembered how beautiful she was as a young girl.

She flew into the great room, her wings in a swirl of ordered flight. In an instant she landed on top of the huge oak table in the corner of the room. With her falcon eyes she observed the surroundings in this massive library room: Books, in carved pageantry, were stacked from floor to ceiling as the bookcases lined the walls. Marble statues of deities and nymphs were on display. The furniture was satin chairs with carved figures galore. The room was alive with art and precious objects of all kind. Even a battle scenes with a knight challenging a dragon to a duel to the death. Many hours Anneto had spent here, learning from the books and just playing with the art forms... it was where her childhood dreams had come to life.

The King and Queen sat upon their throne chairs near the center of the room. Off to the right was a dais, with four oak carved chairs. Sitting in each of the chairs was an Elder Wizard of the Kingdom. The four Elders: two male, two females..were the mages of the kingdom. They controlled all the magic that happened here. When Anneto pleaded with them for the right to raise Fabbo from his death… they agreed..but with the penance that he would be born as bird…and that Anneto must forfeit her presence as a woman, and stay in her falcon form forever. Anneto had the ability to change from woman to bird anytime she wanted. It was a magic gift she received at her birth. To save Fabbo, she decided to give up her female body to be a bird..to be like him and with him all her life. She never once regretted this decision. She loved Fabbo with all her heart. Now they were married and she soon would have her marriage consecrated with their first intimate encounter. Why was she called here..and what was the reason for the four Elders' purpose?

Anneto sat on the perch in the center of the large table and said in a pleading tone. Although she was a falcon she still had her sweet voice to speak with…she looked directly into the eyes of her parents and said, "Why ?…Mom and Dad…why have you brought me back here? Please tell me..as I long to go back to my dear Fabbo…he waits patiently for me!"

King Saygar and Queen Tiva looked at each other and then the King spoke directly to his daughter. "Dearest Anneto, let the Elders answer your question." He pointed to the dais where the four elders sat. Anneto shifted her gaze to them.

The oldest of the Elders..a man with long silver hair. It was shining on his head and beard with a glow like a multitude of little stars that twinkled upon each strand of hair. There was a glow of light that covered the aura of his whole being. He stood and spoke in a mellow yet determined tone;

"Dearest Anneto, we were there when you were born. We gave you the power to change your being into a bird. We wanted you to know what flight felt like. As you are a true angel in your spirit. When you came to us to ask for the life to be restored in that gallant knight. We thought of the price to pay for this impossible wish. We put you to the test…to see if your love was strong enough to withstand the harshness of the choice and to live all your life as a bird. Now we realize the punishment was too strong. You were born a girl, a human being…we should not have taken that away from you… We have decided to rescind our decision.. we can take the spell off of you..and once again, you can be a true woman…for the rest of your life. If you accept, then as it is written… it shall be done."

These words hit Anneto like a bomb exploding in her brain. Secretly, she had longed for herself to be a woman again… to wake up in the morning and see her toes…instead of looking down at her claws. To feel real lips on her mouth…not a curved beak! Oh, to have a woman's body …with its soft curves, its sweet scent, the longing of beautiful legs to walk upon…to have firm pointy breasts that quietly bounced as she ran barefoot across the floor..Oh, how she missed all of this, and now she could have it back.

With a new excitement in her voice she quickly turned to the elders and said… "Oh, I would love to be a woman again…and can you make my Fabbo into a man?"

The Elders conferred with each other for a moment then the older elder stood again and said, "That would be impossible …. He had died and his body was taken away.. his redemption was in the form of an Eagle…his angel spirit has the wings of the known world to

fly in. He must remain an Eagle to survive..
We can grant you human form, but not for him."
Make your choice now.. as it is only given
once.. and that decision is final."

Anneto was torn..she was ripped apart. Should
she become a woman and never see Fabbo
again. As she pondered this life changing
decision. She put her wings over her ears.
Then she realized.. her whole body was
covered with feathers.. She had claws on her
feet. She had a beak instead of a mouth. And
the terrible reality hit her. She was a bird…sure
she could fly..but she wanted long hair instead
of feathers. She wanted to look beautiful.
There were many charming knights in the
king's guard. She remembered when she
passed by their training quarters. They would
be in a mock battle. Stripped to the waist…
their strong muscles steaming in sweet sweat.
How they stopped and bowed to her as she
walked by. How they longed to just look at her.
She was too young to feel anything but
admiration for them. Now she was a woman
and her body would be firm and strong..and
beautiful. She made her decision. Turning to
the Elders she exclaimed in a strong female
voice.

I am so grateful for this gift of my womanhood.
I accept it fully. My thanks to you and the great
forces that guide you…my dearest
elders…accept my deepest love for this gift of
my true-self."

With those words said. "A golden light
appeared in the room. It surrounded Anneto
and filled her full of its power. She began to
transform into the being of a beautiful woman.
Then it was complete. Where a falcon had
been on a perch there now appeared a totally
lovely young lady in its place. The parents and
even the elders were a little surprised.. she
was a woman, but totally naked. As this was
her birth from the spell put upon her ….as if a
child born.. with only her body in its
completeness.

The Queen got up immediately and put the
cape from her gown around her daughter.. She
said in a quiet voice, "Welcome home my
darling." The king approached and put his arm
around his lovely daughter. "I will send a note
to Fabbo and a gift to him. He must not come
here as he would be devastated to be an eagle
and not be able to be with you. He would feel
like your pet..and I think neither of you want
that.

Anneto nodded her head and said, "You are right daddy. I must never see Fabbo again. I will keep his memory in my heart forever.

The Elders left. The Queen took Anneto to her room. The king sat at his desk and wrote a note to Fabbo.
"My Dear once upon a time Son, Anneto will not be coming back to you. She has been given the gift of becoming a woman again. She tried desperately to have you brought back as a knight but it was not possible. I give you a cottage in the Great Forest where you may live and make a life for yourself…This is goodbye forever… know that we will miss you.. and think of you and all the great deeds you have done… thank you ….Saygar, king of Thc Kingdom of the East."

He attached the note to the leg of the carrier pigeon and it flew out the painted portrait glass window on its way to bring the news of this transformation to Fabbo.

Realm of Angels...part 13
(New Beginnings)

It was early morning when Fabbo awoke. The
pigeon carried the note to tell Fabbo that
Anneto had returned to her human body. She
was no longer a Falcon and would not be
coming back to him. He was devastated...
Then to his surprise a trio of singing Meadow
Larks flew onto the balcony. They sang in
unison a series of songs. After they had
serenaded Fabbo the leader of the group
spoke up.

My name is Cherpy "This is a wedding gift from
the King and Queen...he looked over at Fabbo
and smiled.." Anneto's Mom and Dad were
very generous ... they told me to inform you as
a parting gift they bought you a new house!"

Fabbo flew up off of the bed and landed on his
feet..he spoke excitedly..." You have got to be
kidding me..her folks bought me a
house!!...then he added..."can you take me
there to see it?"

Cherpy gave a bird whistle...." sure can, ...just
follow us...it's located at the base of the Great

Mountain. .. next to that little village where 'The Travelers Inn' is located."

Fabbo said. " I know that part of the Great Forest.. It's a special place. That's where the travelers from all over the kingdoms go to find the secret of The Very Last Lost Castle. Even with my flying powers and all the magic I possess I probably could never penetrate that invisible barrier dome that covers the entrance to that magical place. Wow, and now I have our very own home right there at the base of the mountain."

Fabbo reminisced... "When I was a knight I had heard tales of that secret castle at the top of the Great Mountain. Now that I am an Eagle, with my wingspan and flying power, maybe I can penetrate that barrier and see this secret castle for myself."

The meadowlarks started a melodious bird laugh. Chirpy spoke up.." let me tell you many birds have tried to breach that dome..all failed. It's foolproof..the only way in is to crack the code written on the flaming doorway...(Let all Ye who wish to enter find the True and Only Way).. figure that out, and some have, and you are granted entrance to that magic kingdom..for now, let's go look at your new house.``

With that said, the trio of meadowlarks, with Fabbo in tow, took off to fly to see his new home.

They landed just outside the hamlet at the base of the Great Mountain. Chirpy waddled with them to a small office building with a sign that read " Secret Mountain Realty Office".

They went inside. An elderly owl was sitting at the desk. Chirpy chirped up…" Mister Owlie, this is Fabbo…the King and Queen of the East Kingdom bought him a cottage as a parting gift…his marriage to their daughter was annulled."

The elderly owl looked up and said.."oh, yes,pleased to meet you in person. The royal family bought the "bird cottage" sight unseen.I have to tell you first there might be a problem"

All the birds looked surprised..Fabbo spoke up.." What kind of problem are you talking about? Is the house unsafe… with bad plumbing or something like that.

Mr. Owlie spoke quickly…"Oh no, nothing like that. Actually, the cottage is perfect and really beautiful. It has a garden and trees, even a babbling brook that runs next to it. The problem is on the other side of the property is where the swamp is. There is an establishment there called, "The Swamp Duck Saloon". A lot of unsavory birds hang out there…. like drunken ducks, frilly geese, and even some bare breasted chickens who do pole dancing there. The swamp water is fermented. There is alcohol in the fermented vegetation that grows there. The birds and small animals drink this juice and get drunk on it. I tell you this because they will be your neighbors…although there are thick bramble bushes that protect your property from them. You must consent before you sign the lease. I must say, this cottage is so beautiful..yet, it seems to always be up for sale. Maybe the noise won't bother you and if not, this could be a real paradise to live there.

Fabbo thought to himself for a few minutes. Then spoke up.."This is a gift from the royal family…I do not wish to spoil their gift…. I will take it!"

He sighed the papers and the house was his.

He flew to the cottage on graceful wings. From the air he saw the beautiful garden. The flowers seemed to be dancing on their stems as he approached the garden. Just before he landed he caught a glimpse of the "Swamp Duck Saloon" he could almost smell the fermented water that surrounded it. On the porch of the saloon were some tipsy ducks lounging around. One gander was sitting on a rocking chair with a bare breasted chicken sitting on his lap…
Fabbo had heard of a "Lap Dance" before…but not between a chicken and a goose!. He felt a little disgusted but didn't bring it up.

He landed right next to the cottage. The grass was green and the lawn and garden in an immaculate order. The previous owners had kept it in great shape.
He went into the house and it was beautiful. A bowl of birdseed on the dining room table. A gift from the realtor. He was very happy with his new house and garden.

A week went by and now he firmly moved it. No problem with the Swamp Saloon..as the bramble bush was a barrier that kept them safe.

Also those drunken birds kept to themselves. They had no interest in the neighborhood that surrounded the swamp. They came here from all over the forest just to get drunk and have a good time with the moonshine and birdie gals who danced and drank with them.

The neighbors of the Eagle were mostly other birds too. Only of different species. There were two love birds who lived in the cottage nearby. A few Robin redbreasts who were single lady birds..and attended bird college. A singing canary..she was a beautiful bird..many of the sparrows and pigeons were in love with her. There was even an adorable parrot..who spoke several Bird languages. She was a tutor. A really gorgeous bird who was very much attracted to the male species..as she had two hawks that she dated regularly. And a lovely young Eagle. She had graduated from bird college and was ready to make her mark on the kingdom. She had a small cottage down by the babbling brook. No where near the Swamp Duck Saloon.

All was going well, except for one thing. It seemed every female bird in this part of the kingdom was attracted to Fabbo. He was so generous with his time and effort to help whenever someone needed something…and it seemed, all these female flying creatures needed his attention all the time, he was there for them.

Still, he seemed to be attracted to "Cintas" The young single female Eagle. She was enamored by his great looks and flying ability. Love was brewing here. It was just a matter of time before he would ask for her wings in marriage.

At first Cintas didn't mind all the attention the other female birds were giving to Fabbo. Now, she felt a little jealous.."he never sang that Eagle song for me!"
She said to herself. She was getting a little depressed that he was paying so much attention to those other female birdies.

Then, one night when Fabbo was fast asleep she decided she needed an adventure on her own. She put on a bird perfume that she sprayed under her feathers. It made her female species very desirable.

She said to herself, " I just want to feel very feminine tonight. Then, she slipped out of the cottage and flew over the bramble bush the was the protective barrier between her house and the Swamp Duck Saloon.

As soon as she landed there she realized she had made a mistake. She turned around and was ready to fly back over the bramble bush to the safety of her home…when she heard a voice.

" Well, well, what have we here..is that a beautiful young Eagle I see… or are my eyes deceiving me?"

She turned around and stared into the eyes of a large dark vulture.

Before she could say anything.. he reached out and grabbed her wing. He did not let go while he talked.

"My name is Spike. I'm the bouncer here at the Drunk Duck Saloon" he snickered .."That's what I call it anyway". ..he rambled in a low voice…"Spike, the Vulture..that's me, and I promise I won't let anything bad happen to you!"

Still holding onto her wing he pulled her into the bar. She wanted to refuse..but he was very persuasive.

He yelled to the bartender..a frog with a cap on his head that said.."I'm a Prince- kiss me!"

"Hey Foggy…Give the lady a drink..it's on me!"

He finally let go of her wing and said…"I know this is your first time here..have a drink on my..you enjoy yourself..I got to go back to work."

Cintas saw the glass of fermented swamp water that was on the bar before her. She thought to herself.."oh, well, you only live once, here goes"…and she took a sip of the fermented drink. Surprisingly it tasted pretty good..it had a tangy sort of sweet smell to it. She gulped down half the drink with the next sip.

Sitting on the seat next to her was a drunken female duck. She gave a sort of a smile and handed a damp feathered wing tip to her.

"Let me introduce myself..I'm Freeda the Swamp Duck. I have slept with every kind of bird you can think of…I also bedded with Squirrels, chipmunks, and even a Skunk who claimed he was a prince in another lifetime! I'm not really from here. I live in another fairy tale but I like to travel to the Swamp Saloon wherever it exists. Let me buy you a drink sweetie."

Freeda waved her feathers at the bartender and he came over with two swamp cocktails in his hands.
He gave one to Freeda and the other one to Cintas.

With a "cheers" Freeda chugged it down..she turned to the slightly tipsy Eagle and said.."bottoms up baby!"

Without thinking Cintas chugged her swamp juice down in one gulp!

Foggy gave a whistle and said.." wow, you are princess in disguise…if you give me a little kiss, I got another drink for you on the house!" Then he pointed to his cap..give it a try- and a prince may appear."

Cintas thought about it and said.."I never kissed a frog before..maybe I will give it a try...just this once!"

She leaned over and Foggy put his lips right on her beak. It turned out to be a long soulful kiss..
Centas finally pulled away and said..."You are not a frog...you're a horny toad!" They all laughed at that one.
Foggy then brought over another round of drinks! While they were laughing and giggling the door opened and Spike the Vulture came into the bar.

He scampered over and gave Freeda a big vulture sized kiss. Then he turned to Cintas and said , " Hey, sweet Eagle gal I see you are still here. I have a room at the back of this joint. Why don't you come back there and join me for a drink."

Cintas looked at him. She was feeling very woozy as the fermented drinks were getting to her. She said in a slurred voice.."I don't think that is such a good idea."

Spike said.."Sure it is!"..he grabbed her by the wing and guided her up off of the barstool. She didn't really resist him. She said.." Well, just one drink then I have to go home...it's getting late."

Spike the Vulture said…"One drink it is"...then he nudged her toward the back of the room where his room was located…

Spike poured the swamp juice into a large glass and handed it to Cintas.
She protested…"Hey, you said one drink…this is huge!"

As soon as Spike heard her say that he took the drink out of her hand and pushed her down on the bed.

She yelled, ``Stop, what are you doing?"

He lay on top of her and in a breathy tone.." You came up to my room..you took my drink..now you want to take me in your bed...isn't that right!"

Cintas was confused. She did go willingly to his room and took his drink..her head was spinning from the fermented swamp juice…she said ... "yes!"... but before she could finish her sentence telling him it was just for a drink…he was upon her. It was just a blur of images after that.

And then it was over. She got up off the bed, tears in her young eagle eyes. She flew as fast as she could out of the bar and over the bramble bushes.

Fabbo had gotten up early that morning as the Sun was just starting to rise. Cintas flew blindly and ended up almost upon him. She bounced off the porch and landed hard on the ground.

He flew over and knelt beside her. She looked up, saw him, and blurted out everything that happened to her.

He looked into her eyes and said, " I have loved you from the first moment I saw you. Today you will be my wife. If you will have me as your husband I shall love and cherish you all the days of my life.

Cintas looked up. The tears in her eyes were replaced by the glow of happiness. "Yes, oh Yes, dear sweet Fabbo..I will be your bride. Hold me in your great wings..as I am yours, forever.

Realm of Angels...part 14
(The Consequence)

Cintas the beautiful young Eagle had gotten herself in a lot of trouble. She had gone to "The Swamp Duck Saloon" and drank fermented swamp juice...then ended up having an encounter with Spike the Vulture. She was devastated and embarrassed. Fabbo the Eagle came to her rescue and promised to marry her. All this was going through her mind as she lay upon the porch of Fabbo's cottage..."Will he really marry me?" This thought went through her eagle brain.

Then, reality set in as soon as Fabbo spoke.... "Dearest Cintas, I can imagine what you went through when you decided to go see what that Swamp Saloon was all about . It's over now. Tomorrow as soon as the sun rises I will take you to the mayor of "Travelers Village" . He is also an official who can marry us. I have loved you from the moment I saw you. You are an Eagle like me...If you accept me I promised to love and cherish you."

Cintas opened her eyes wide and said, "Yes, Please marry me. I love you too!!"

The Sun rose almost by command and the two Eagles flew over the trees to the Travelers village. It was just sunrise. The people and animals there were just getting up...some going to work. It was a prosperous village with people, elves, and animals working and playing side by side. Such a happy place.

In the center of this village was a large marble fountain with a stone statue of the Princess who was the monarch of the Very Last Lost Castle. The fabled castle at the top of the Great Mountain. No one had ever seen the Princess, all they knew were the rumors they had heard from the travelers who came to solve the mountain's mystery. A dove with golden wings would fly all over the kingdoms and invite special one's it selected to come to the mountain and meet the princess.. whose name was known as, Ablaze Brightly.

If they solved the riddles she imposed to find the way...they could reach the castle and she would grant them one supreme wish. Anything that they could think of was available to them with this one wish...all that was required of the person, animal, creature, or bird that made it this far was that the wish be one that they desired above all others…If the Princess deemed it worthy she would grant it . If not, then the traveler had made the trip in vain..

Fabbo and Cintas went to the town hall. The mayor, who was a wise old owl was there in her
office. She was a gracious owl named "Hoota" and had been mayor for a long time. Although quiet by nature she was very loud when she made decisions. Fabbo approached her . "Dear Mayor, I wish to marry this wonderful Eagle...can you do this honor for us?"

Hoota, put on her spectacles. She was nearsighted, which was unusual because her night vision was great...but the daylight was a bit too strong for her to concentrate on documents that needed to be signed.

She replied, "Who will give away the bride? Do you have a bouquet and a ring?"

Fabbo was flabbergasted, he said with an apologetic tone..."Ah, no …this is a wedding we just decided on last night."
Hoota interrupted, "No matter, we can provide everything"…she gave a few loud hoots and some elves appeared with all the proper items

and the wedding when on. After it was over Fabbo kissed his new bride and turned to the mayor and said… "What is the charge for the beautiful ceremony you have performed?" Hoota smiled and said, "To get married is free, the price you pay is to be faithful to your bride. That will be the best gift you can give to her."

Fibbo turned to Cintas and said… "I pledge my love to you. I promise to make you happy and provide for you" Cintas looked at her new husband and with happy tears in her eyes she said, " I love you dearly and promise you from the bottom of my heart to make you happy." Then, their wings enclosed upon each other and they embraced in a moment of total happiness.

They went back to Fabbo's cottage. The next day Cintas sold her little house and moved in for good. A week went by and in the morning Cintas woke Fabbo up to tell him the news ….. "My dearest husband, I must tell you…I am with child." Fibbo was so happy…he flew into the sky and did acrobatic twists and turns in the cloudless sky.

Still, something bothered Cintas…she thought back to the time of her conception and it was the day she wandered to the Swamp Saloon. She vaguely remembered the encounter with Spike the Vulture… then she dismissed the idea.. "that could never be?" She fought off the thought.

Thirty five days on the calendar…the Stork midwife was there to help in the delivery. Fabbo was in the other room and heard his wife going through the birth ritual. Then the Stork came out of the room and said to him …."Congratulations…it's a boy"..then, with a disgusted look on her face… "Yes, it's a boy.. but it's a baby Vulture!.. You should keep track of what your wife does when she is not with you"… with that said she just fled from the cottage not even waiting to ask for any compensation for her work in the delivery.

Fabbo went into the bedroom and there was Cintas with a baby vulture clutched in her wings; She looked longingly at Fabbo and said, "I am so sorry…but this is my son, I gave birth to him. I shall love and take care of him. Please forgive me for the terrible mistake I made." With that said, the tears flooded from her eyes and fell upon the baby vulture who clung to his mommy. It was mother and child in a loving embrace.

Fabbo came to the bed and knelt beside it. He bowed to his wife and said...."I shall accept the child as if it were my own. It will be our son, together. I shall love him as you do. We will bring him up together "...with that said they embraced, father, mother, and son... in a loving moment of happiness.

Weeks went by and the baby vulture grew...Most of the other birds shunned him. They made him feel like an outcast. Still he grew to be a young strong vulture. He went to bird school and the young birds didn't shun him anymore...he wouldn't let them. He became a bully in school. He was bigger than the other birds. He made them give him their birdseed and he pushed them around and got whatever he wanted.

The teachers were afraid of him. The called Cintas and Fabbo into the school office to tell them their son was a total bully. Even they couldn't control him. He knew he was a big dark bird with carnivore needs. He was just a bad bird.... Still his parents forgave him.. and cared for him.

Then one night when his wings were full grown he flew over the bramble bushes and went into the Swamp Duck Saloon. As soon as the bouncer, Spike the Vulture, saw him he said… "You are my Son…Vulchy recognized his species immediately and ran up to Spike and said…"You are my real dad, aren't you!"

The next day Fabbo and Cintas got a notice from the mayor judge at town hall that Vulchy wanted to be with his real father…and it was a court order that was granted.

That afternoon Spike flew over the brambles to land on the front porch of Fabbo's house. Vulchy was waiting for him. There were tears in Cintas eyes..she couldn't bear to loose her son. Spike looked at her and said, …"See the good thing that came out of our only fling..you gave me a son.' With those words said, Spike and his vulture son flew over the bramble bushes never to be seen again on this side of the forest.

It was then that Fabbo made up his mind. He and Cintas would leave their home and make the trek up the mountain to find the princess

Ablaze Brightly…and give her their one secret
wish.. to have a child of their own…fBk

Realm of Angels…part 15
(The Miracle)

Cintas was still devastated by the loss of her
son. Yes, he was the result of a forced affair,
still she loved him as her only child. Now Spike
the Vulture came to claim his son..and the
young vulture went with him willingly. Fabbo
had tried his best to be a father to this
unfortunate child .. but the vulture in the boy
was too strong and he chose to be in the wild
with his true father. Now they were free to try to
solve the mystery of the Very Last Lost Castle.
The mystical castle of Princess Ablaze Brightly
who ruled her domain in magic and mystery.

The two Eagles left their home and only took
their love with them. They flew high in the sky
and circled the great transparent dome that
surrounded the inner part of the Great Forest.
This time they used their eagle eyes to
penetrate all the surroundings.. and there it
was…hidden behind a pair of weeping willow
trees… the magic entrance. The trees had a

natural bend to their branches so it was almost impossible to see the doorway. It was covered with leaves until it was noticed..only then, once discovered, would it produce its wreath of flaming embers that lit up the inscription above its doorway…"Let all Ye who wish to enter-find the True and Only Way." They landed in front of the doorway and embraced in each other's wings..Fabbo spoke in a fervent tone.."The only thing we offer to enter is our undying love for each other."

A deep mellow voice spoke from the doorway …."That is the secret that opens the way to the Lost Castle.. as only with true love can it be found "…with those words spoken the doorway opened and Fabbo and Cintas passed through. The first thlng they noticed was how beautiful it was within the protective dome. The trees swayed as if they were alive. The flowers were singing. Small animals hopping around in glee. This was a magic place to be.

The two Eagles had a big advantage over all the other travelers who sought to find the path to the peak of the Great Mountain…where the Castle of Princess Ablaze Brightly was located. They didn't have to trudge up the mountain path and meet all the obstacles on the way. They were Eagles with strong wings.. They flew up into the sky and made their way over the few villages and hamlets that surrounded the mountain ..they flew over the hills and boulders and mountain streams and landed directly on the courtyard of the Very Last Lost Castle. Princess Brightly was in the garden. She was singing to her weeping willow trees. They were always in tears.. not from sadness but from joy to listen to the beautiful voice of the Princess. The two eagles landed on the golden fountain .. it was made of solid gold with carvings of angels with trumpets..as if playing a heavenly serenade.

As soon as Fabbo and Cintas landed, Princes Ablaze turned to them and said in a soft melodic voice. "I have been watching you two for a long time. Such trials and tribulations you have encountered. I commend you on your perseverance..yes, you made it here. I know your request...but there are reservations and penalties that must be paid. You must atone for the spell that was put upon you."

She paused, then continued with a serious tone to her voice… "Fabbo, you were once a Knight and champion warrior. What I will grant for you..is to give you your life back in your human form. You will be a Woodsman and live in a cabin here at the center of the mountain. You will build small homes for the animals and birds to live in… you will be a writer of their tales. It is here that you will find your ultimate happiness. As it is written …a child will come to you..with all its mysteries.

Then she turned to Cintas and said…"You are a true Eagle…I cannot make you a human … but what I can do for you is grant you the freedom to fly anywhere within or outside of the Great Forest. Your mission will be to find the starving and neglected children. You will comfort them and bring happiness to their tears..Yes, you will be the mother to many children..of all species..they will love you very much…as you will be the mother that they seek so dearly…If you agree to this then it shall be done… your marriage will be over.. as you will be of different forms.. a bird and a human.. if you accept this then your love will not be lost in vain."

Fabbo and Cintas looked deeply into each other's eyes and bowed.. then they looked at the princess and said… "We accept our Fate".

The transformation was immediate…without saying another word to each other, they turned and began their new journey. Fabbo went to the deep forest and began to build his log cabin.

Cintas flew into the sky …she had a mission to fulfill. Each night Fabbo would talk in his dreams. He told about his love for Anneto..how she was a human woman before she gave it up for him to spend the rest of her life as a Falcon. How she was given the right to be a female person again.. and she took it..and left Fabbo to be with her parents the King and Queen of the East Kingdom.

Cintas flew out of the dome over the valleys and streams. She saw the tower of the East KIngdom. The sentry guards were on duty but this night they were related, some even slightly sleeping on duty. Cintas silently flew into the tower window of Anneto's bedroom. The princess was lying on her bed softly sobbing. Cintas landed right on the bed and startled the princess.. she spoke quickly… "Dear Anneto I know who you are… Fabbo spoke of you in his dreams every night. I am here because he has regained his human body and I tell you this to see if you still have feelings for him."

Anneto wiped the tears from her eyes and said…I have cried myself to sleep every night just thinking about him. My love for him is so strong that I cry everyday to his memory. All the knights here want to romance me but I am still a virgin as my love only belongs to Fabbo."

Cintas said, "I am endowed with magical strength. Take your hands and wrap them firmly around my legs. I will carry you to the Great Forest and to Fabbo. Leave a note for your parents that you will be safe and this is your choice for your duty to Love's Wishes."

Anneto wrote the note and she grabbed onto Cintas with all her might. They flew over the dome and onto the ground where Fabbo was building his log cabin. The moment he saw her his heart leaped with joy. They embraced and after a long kiss… Fabbo said, "We must get married again!"

Anneto said, "No need… I didn't let daddy destroy our marriage certificate…it was tucked in a pouch around her neck…they embraced in love's riches all night long… exactly nine months later…Anneto gave birth to a beautiful baby girl.. she was perfect in all ways..except one.. she had a lovely pair of wings..they had a baby angel …and the whole Great Mountain rejoiced when they heard the news.

This is the happy ending to their story.. but it is the beginning of the Angel-tale of "Fabszy and Rosie".. the fallen angels who lost their wings..and now it is their turn to find the way to true destiny"s call…

****

Realm of Angels…. part 16
(The Fallen Angels)

Time has a way of standing still. Especially in the dome of the Great Forest. Characters who enter will sometimes go into a state of suspended animation. They freeze in place till fate figures out their story.

This happened to Fabszy and Rosie. As soon as they pledged their undying love for each other...the magic portal opened and welcomed them in. Then, they stayed suspended in time until this moment when Fate let them pass to find their goal.

As soon as Fabszy opened his eyes he remembered all that had happened to him. He was an Angel of deep desire who had fallen in love with Rosie, the angel of goodness. Together their love had brought them to middle ground…one of love and desire in unison. The price both paid for crossing the barrier between light and dark was to lose the flight of their wings. Now their wings, with the tips cut off lay upon their backs as a bundle of tangled feathers. They carried this heavy weight upon their backs as punishment for their desire of love's wants and wishes.

Now Rosie awoke and she came to the same realization as her lover. They looked at each other. The once proud beautiful angels with magnificent wings…now their wings lay as a bundle of tangled feathers upon their backs.

They walked along a deserted path that led them to a small hamlet. It was noontime and some children were playing upon the grass that adorned the path. As soon as the children saw them they started laughing. When they walked by, a cheerful little boy said in a low tone… "Wow, look at them.. they are hunchbacks!" The other children just giggled under their breath.

This made both Fabszy and Rosie very uncomfortable. They looked at each other and realized their dead wings did make them look like they had humps on their backs. Then the frightening realization came to them…their wings had a will of their own. They could actually move upon their backs. The dead wings could make themselves into a ball and look like a hump on their body, or, they could straighten themselves out and look like a long feather cape. It seemed their wings had a mind of their own….and it was beyond their control. They fought the behavior of their wings all they way to the front desk of the "Travelers Inn".

Sitting behind the welcome sign check-in desk was a middle aged woman with a smiling face. She immediately put down the shawl that she was knitting and placed her hands on the counter top. She spoke with a friendly tone.

"I wasn't expecting any travelers today. We have some small animals around here that are just too happy to let me know when travelers are arriving. You two must have come through the portal without much fanfare. Usually those who make it through there are so excited they yell and scream for joy. Anyway, welcome to the Travelers Inn..will you be wishing for one room or two?"

Fabszy and Rosie were surprised by this greeting..they just looked at each other. Finally, Fabszy spoke, "We are not yet married but we wish to be as soon as possible!

He turned to Rosie's and sort of whispered..."Is it ok if I ask for one room...I want you near me till we find a 'Justice of the Peace' to marry us."

Rosie nodded ok...The clerk spoke again.." I'm glad you chose The Travelers Inn over The Forest Edge Lodge...they usually get most of the business. It's owned by the Mayor and his wife. This place is all mine...by the way, the Mayor's wife is my sister. Her husband does perform marriage ceremonies. I heard you mention you want to get married. Well, if you need a bridesmaid I'm available."

Rosie perked up.."Yes, yes, thank you...that would be wonderful. We will need everything for our wedding. We left all we had behind when we entered the portal.

The Traveler Inn owner, whose name was Gizzy, gave a whistle..."Wow! That could be expensive. What do you have to barter for all that?"

Rosie, reached into her Fanny pack that she kept tied to her slim waist. She opened the zippered compartment and pulled out a handful of currency. She said in an excited voice.." These are Angel coins. They are made of solid 24 karat gold. They have an unusual quantity "…she tossed one coin in the air..the golden wings on the surface of the coin came alive..they began to flutter and the coin flew through the air. It landed right in the palm of Gizzy's hand. She enclosed it in her palm and said.."A few of these will get you whatever you need to have a great wedding!"

With that said she gave them the key to the best room at the Inn.
"Have a good night"…she said, then followed it with.."I will contact the Mayor and have everything ready for you by tomorrow afternoon."

With the key in his hand Fabszy and Rosie went to the deluxe room. They would make it their bridal suite.

As soon as they entered the room Fabszy took his bride to be in his arms and planted a loving kiss on her startled mouth. She blushed slightly then smiled…"That will be all we can do for now..I am very dusty from our trip here. What I need is a refreshing shower...then we can continue where our kiss left off."

She smiled shyly, then sort of danced her way across the room to where the shower was located. She turned on the warm water and let her tunic fall to the floor.
She was dazzlingly beautiful in her nakedness. Even her dead wings seemed to sense this as they huddled shyly upon her back.

She left the curtain open as she stepped into the shower. She let the welcoming warm water tingle upon her face and hair as it dripped down her body washing away any debris that dared lay upon it.

Then, an extraordinary thing happened. The dead wings upon her back seemed to come alive. They formed an umbrella over her head. The warm shower water bounced off of it as if it was a rain shower outside.

Rosie gave a giggle in glee. She spoke with a joyful tone.." Look, my dead wings are trying to protect me. They cannot fly but they seem to think it's their job to keep me safe!"

She reached up and began talking to her wings..."oh great wings that have granted me flight. You must listen to me..this shower is for my own good. It will make me feel clean and refreshed. Please let the water cleanse me."

The wings seemed to understand. They immediately dropped down and fell into a ball that appeared to rise up from the back of her neck and swirl itself into a pompadour on top of her head.

Rosie laughed.." Look, it has given me a new hairstyle...I have a crown of feathers on my head!"

They both laughed at that one . With a bottle of soap lotion that was there. She poured some into her beautiful soft hand..and began to rub it upon her body.

Fabszy who had been watching this private bath ritual now became so mesmerized by her beauty that his body tingled with excitement.

He let his tunic drop and he stood there facing her in the complete honesty of his manly body.

She looked up from her washing and was shocked to see him in all his glory. She had never seen a male body in its total completeness in person. She had only imagined what a male might look like without the restrictions of clothing. This, she was not prepared for…the honesty and beauty of the male body in its entirety. So strong and powerful the muscles. So regal the stance of its grace. So desirable to reach out and touch its sensuality.

For a moment all time stopped…he opened his arms to her…begging, almost pleading, that she come to him and let their warm bodies meet in an embrace.

She sensed this in him, and gave In completely. She stepped out of the shower and ran into his open arms.

A moment before she got there her right wing came up over her shoulder and smacked Fabszy right in the face. The force of the blow almost knocked him off of his feet.

He finally recovered with a shocked look on his face. He tried to advance toward Rosie…when her wings came up over both of her shoulders and formed a protective feathery cage around her body.

Fabszy spoke in a startled voice…"your dead wings are now alive…they cannot provide flight…but they are determined to protect you at all cost. To them, you are a virgin and they won't let you do anything to threaten that privilege!"

As he was talking he felt his dead wings come alive. They pushed him forward and began to nudge open Rosie's wings. For a moment the two pairs of wings were battling each other. She is a virgin from the moderate Realm. He, an Angel of desire from the Deep Desires realm of Angels. So different in needs yet a middle ground these two had reached on all things except sensual contact.

When they realized this they both pushed backwards and their wings relaxed in peace.

Fabszy said, "I realize now our wings will not permit any sexual contact without fighting each other. We must wait till our wedding to resolve this issue."

Rosie bowed her head in agreement.

Fabszy, with a determined look on his face, spoke in a solemn tone..
I will write a poem to you here and now to pledge my love to you. With that said, he took his magic quill…and began his poem to her.

My desperate Love

What is this that drives me so?
To give you a love that you don't know.
To touch you where one has never been.
With purity of heart is this a forgiven sin?

My desire is beyond my control.
Upon your body I wish to enroll.
To ride with you in a golden carriage;
As my wife, in a sacred marriage.

What must I do to tell your wings;
My desire is with cheers and sings…
Let me take Rosie as my bride;
The love we have- we cannot hide.

Please, dear wings of flights of death;

Let me love Rosie with each breath.
Tomorrow we marry to be as one;
It is then our new life will have begun…
(Fibby Bob Kinney (c) .

He handed her the poem to read. As she did her wings tried to rise up on her back and grab the poem out of her hands.

She reached back and slapped the wings..then proclaimed.." Haven't you done enough already..you have kept us apart with your pious feelings. Do you not understand how much I love Fabszy?"

The wings cowered upon her back as if ashamed of themselves. Rosie continued to read the poem. When she finished there was a deep look of love in her eyes. She spoke softly and with a hush in her voice, as if she didn't want her wings to hear what she was saying…"My sweet angel…your poem has moved me greatly..now I shall write my poem to you..it will tell the deep feelings in my heart… which I give to you completely."

With that said, she took her golden quill and began to write her poem to Fabszy.

"Passion and Purity"
My dearest Fabszy,

If there's anything I desire to make you whole
It's my whole self - my body, my heart and
soul.
I have waited for so long for you to take all my
charms
To surrender everything to you- my lips , and
my arms
To feel the ecstasy of having our bodies
entwined
To be enthralled in fiery passion, yet so
sublime

But fate has made us wait longer than we
should
Many gargantuan hurdles we had conquered
Likened to climbing high steepy mountains
Swimming thru enormous waves of oceans
Surviving courageously tempestous storms.
Finally , we are together, no fear of separation

We can build our own quiet and happy home
Yet, as husband and wife, elusive is our union.
Tomorrow we shall see finally wed
I can accept you in my bed
We can realize our deepest dreams

Our love will remain supreme.
(Fe Rosario V. Maximo (c)

Fabszy with tears in his eyes..took the poem
she had written and pressed it to his lips.

"Tomorrow, my darling we will be wed. I will
kiss your body till tears of joy flow from your
eyes. I will love you as I do this poem you
wrote to me now. I will sleep with it upon my
pillow..as the scent of you is in its core..as in all
of you I do adore.

They both slept sweetly as the reverence of
their marriage danced in their dreams.

Realm of Angels …part 17
(The Almost Wedding)

Now that they knew their once dead wings
were in charge of their emotions. With the use
of their body they became more cautious. They
kissed gently and were dressed in full length
pajamas that were part of a room service
package. They got into the king size

bed…careful not to touch each other. Rosie's protective wings watched every move Fabszy made. The stars were bright that night…the Moon very full and watching them from its perch high in the sky. They looked at each other longingly until sleep finally came and took them to dreamland.

The early morning Sun nudged its way over the windowsill of their deluxe room window. With it, the birds were chirping what sounded like "It's a lovely day" and to the fallen angel couple it sure was…this in all its glory would be their wedding day. They dressed quickly. The humps of dead wing feathers, now not active, lay on their backs as lumps of bundled debris; visible through the soft material of their tunics. They walked out of the door and went down the path that led to a sweet Gingerbread House. It was made out of gingerbread and dark chocolate. Somehow they made the bricks so strong that they could withstand the weather and not be bothered by it. They walked in the milk chocolate door which was reinforced with striped candy cane beams. How clever to make a breakfast cafe out of Pastries that were treated to be weather resistant.

When they walked through the door...heads turned. Then, snickers started. These two former angels, handsome and beautiful, still, with visible humps on their backs... the image was overpowering... beauty and grotesque combined in one image... hard to comprehend .

They sat and a waitress came over with a huge smile on her face. She handed them both a menu and took the pencil from behind her ear and placed it on the pad she was holding in her hand ..she said, "Are you ready to order?

Fabszy and Rosie quickly looked at the menu...Fabszy said , "I will take the breakfast special." Rosie nodded, and said, "I will take the same."

The waitress wrote down the order then looked at them and said..."We don't get to see very many fallen angels around here. You must have done something really bad to get your wing tips cut off?"

Fabszy looked at her and said in a sorrowful voice... "Sometimes Fate works in strange ways. We are fallen angels but not of our making. We must live with the burdens that are put upon us."

On her way back to the kitchen the waitress turned and said, "Well if you are lucky enough to solve the puzzles and get to see Princess Ablaze Brightly she may fix those humpy wing tips for you."….with that said, she disappeared into the kitchen.

The angel couple ate their breakfast quietly … then went to City Hall. The Mayor and his wife were already there waiting for them. Lofty, the Mayor, reached out his hand to greet them. "Hello there, You are really the first. Two angels with disabled wings….and, he added quickly, ``You are about to be married… on this …I greatly congratulate you."

His wife who had been standing next to him spoke cheerfully ...."I am "Sprinkles' '…My husband is Mayor, I am the owner of "The Swann Inn' ' it is a wonderful restaurant and wedding chapel. Some of the travelers who pass here end up finding a mate and we marry them cheerfully. I have planned a wonderful wedding for you. My sister Gizzy told me you have angel coins…they are very rare. I think just three of them will cover all the expenses for the entire wedding."

With that said, Rosie reached into her Fanny pack and pulled out three angel coins... they flew into the air on their golden wings and flew right into the outstretched palm of Sprinkles. Lofty, the Mayor, reached to take them but the coins flew into the pocket on Sprinkles' apron... she gave a laugh and said... "See, they know where to go!...now let's get this angel couple ready for their marriage.

A group of elves appeared and took the couple to the wedding boutique down the street. There they picked out a beautiful lace gown for Rosie..and a magnificent tuxedo for Fabszy. The bakers came to the wedding chapel with a giant wedding cake. The table was set for the happy couple. Some of the townspeople were invited to the wedding. They came with their children. This time all was solemn. Even the young children were happy for the fallen angel couple...despite the beautiful gown and tuxedo...the humped wings were still visible beneath all the glamor.

The wedding was on... Gizzy with the bouquet of flowers... an elf band playing the wedding

march. The Mayor in his white suit and tie…he looked very distinguished. There was a dashing Knight in the village… he had come to see the Princess Brightly and volunteered to be the best man. He was stunning in his full suit of armor. Fabszy had purchased a beautiful diamond ring from the town jeweler…When the jeweler found out Fabszy was an angel poet he was so honored by that fact he traded the diamond ring for one of Fabszy's poems…
Which he wrote on the spot …

"Mr. Precious the jeweler":

How wonderful it is for me,
A diamond ring to see.
One for my maiden's hand,
To have my love on demand.

How lucky in this magical place,
Where former sins can be erased.
To seek the princes of magic's will,
A promise for us to fulfill.

I wed today the angel of my dreams;
Together we have met many extremes.
My love to her I give it all;
Together our life to enthrall.

Find me in this dream come true.
I stand here beneath a sky of blue.
To thank "Mr. Precious from my heart;
The ring he gave me -my marriage to start.
Fibby Bob Kinney (c)

Fabszy handed the poem to Mr. Precious who was very grateful. With a tear in his eye he said… "This poem is a treasure I will always keep. It is worth more to me than diamonds and gold. I shall frame it and mount it on my mantle. Every day of my life I can see what an angel gave to me… this is a dear treasure…

Fabszy nodded a thank you… and went back to the wedding chapel… It was time for the ceremony to begin. He gave the ring to the knight who was his best man and they stood there with the Mayor waiting for the bride to walk down the aisle…and there she was… so magnificent and beautiful … two doves sat on her shoulders and children threw flower petals at her feet. She approached the Mayor who held the marriage certificate in his hands. This was a very simple ceremony …all they needed to do was pledge their love to each other and they would become married.

They stood in front of the Mayor and as soon as he said, 'Fabszy, do you take Rosie to be your wife'…Rosie's wings shot up from beneath the neckline of her dress and slapped the wedding certificate out of the Mayor's hand. They turned and tried to attack Fabszy. His wings flew up from his tuxedo collar, nearly ripping the shirt from his body. The two sets of wings were furiously fighting each other.

The Knight who was the best man drew his sword and tried to intervene. The wings knocked the sword from his hand and threw him against the wall. His armor clamored like a pile of junk being tossed upon the floor. The townspeople scampered for their lives. It was a total riot and the chapel was damaged badly. It took five gold coins to take care of the damages. Which left her with only two coins in her fanny pack. The Knight got up from his mangled armor and handed Fabszy back his diamond ring. He said, "Sorry this turned out so badly. Perhaps if you get to see princess Brightly…she will make things right for you. He bowed to them both and left.

The Mayor came over and said with a sad face… "I see your wings will not allow you to marry. This is unfortunate. WIthout their wing tips they felt very bitter and their frustration was building inside of them.

The Mayor spoke…"You can stay here in the chapel overnight but in the morning you must try to see Princess Brightly …she is the only one that can help you now. First, there is one more test you must pass…that is to see the Ogre that guards the entrance to her castle. You must satisfy and pass his test before he will grant you passage to the castle gate. Good luck many a traveler has tried and ended up as a pile of bones in his dungeon cage. Many a knight has come here to challenge him.. as is the case of the one who was your best man.. .they all ended up as his trophy with their sword and helmet hanging on his cave wall. Go and solve the riddle and only then will you find peace and happiness."

With that said he and his wife were gone.. They were alone now …Fabszy showed the ring to Rosie and told her the story of how he had to write a poem to get it… she looked at him and said, "And now I will write a poem to you to prove how strong my love burns in my heart." With that said, she took her quill and began her poem to Fabszy….

"To My Darling Lover"

Like a dream that has no fulfilling ending
Leaving us needing more, always yearning
I thirst for your love to quench my needing
Just as you ardently desire my whole being.

Now that we have thought we have the right
To be one, our powerful wings have made a
fight
Pulling us away from each other's communion
Until sanctification of our marriage is done.

My love, the only one, we had waited so long,
A little more patience waiting we can prolong.
Ardous passion must be subdued for a little
while
Restrained desires endured, purity must prevail
in our trial.
(Fe Rosario V. Maximo (c)

She handed the poem to Fabszy. He placed it
in a pouch around his neck and said…"Let us
go find this ogre and solve his puzzle..it is only
them when we meet Princess Ablaze Brightly
will we find our happiness."

With that said they walked out of the wrecked
wedding chapel..and continued on their journey
to find their happiness…with this parting
remark…from Fabszy.

"I, your angel lost lover..will never leave you till I solve the mystery ..and we can enjoy our togetherness!!!...fBK

Realm of Angels...part 18
(The Ogre's Trail)

With their wedding outfits traded in for some hiking clothes they were ready for the trek up the mountain.
The weather was cool and the journey would be treacherous. They were ready. Nothing would stop their determination to be wed ..and finally share their intimacy with each others body.

A quick meal at the Swann Inn breakfast bar. So delicious was the smell of pancakes and honey syrup...with fresh strawberries and fruitcake dessert. They filled their bellies full...not knowing when their next meal would be.

At the outskirts of the village they came to two paths. Both looked like they went up the mountain. Fabszy remembers that Gizzy, in a passing remark, mentioned that so many travelers had chosen the wrong path and ended outside the protective doom..never allowed to enter the hidden kingdom again.

Now here they were …facing their first challenge. They studied both paths. Each one seemed to go straight up the mountain. There was a wooden sign on a pole placed between the two paths it read…" Choose carefully…to find the correct one to trodden upon .. there is no turning back.. as your destiny will be chosen with your first step."

The two angels looked at each other. Rosie spoke first…"both paths are equally trodden… and the vegetation seems to be the same. Where is the clue on which way to go?"

Fabszy said.."let Nature show us the way. He had kept some fresh bread from the breakfast in his pack. He took out a few pieces and spread them on the ground before him. Then he gave a trilling whistle…a flock of birds that were hidden in the trees on the path to the right…flew from their silent perch and landed at Fabszy's feet. They gobbled up the bread crumbs and flew back into the dense tree tops on the path to the right.

Rosie smiled, "You are a clever Angel. There are no birds on the path to the left. It will lead to empty promises as the bushes whisper the travelers on ..only to lead them where no life is there and they end up nowhere."

Fabszy smiled..." Those who don't use their wits have a fifty-fifty chance of making the right choice. Still, they can only count on Luck for so long to make the right choice. One must find a way to solve the riddle before they can put the test behind them."

With that said…they both stepped upon the path to the right..and continued their journey up the mountain.

The path wove its way past babbling brooks and fields of swaying flowers. So beautiful was this scenery of Mother Nature at her best. Even the small animals were willing to romp and play with these two determined angels.

It was a magical wonderland of fun and frolic.

Rosie, who had felt totally free for the first time since their existence together. They had been through so much…and always the pressure and pain of events left them longing.

They romped and played all day. Fresh berries and fruits of all kinds grew in bushes and trees that were happy to share their goodies with them.

Now it was night. They lay on the soft grass and looked up into the sky. Millions of stars twinkled down upon them. The Moon swayed as upon an invisible hammock in the night sky. They lay close to each other…even their protective wings responded serenely as they lay there in a peaceful sleep.

In the morning the birds awoke them. They carried berries and small fruits on their feet. They dropped their tidbits as breakfast for the two angels.

After they ate Rosie said…I saw a pool of fresh water behind those trees. I will go bathe myself."

Fabszy replied…"while you bathe I shall investigate this area. There might be a hill where I can see further up the mountain."

Rosie went behind the trees and stripped down to go into the water. She had on a hunting shirt and jodhpurs…and leather riding boots. A strange outfit for an Angel to wear but they told her at the boutique it would do well on the trail up the path to the Very Last Lost Castle.

She cast off her clothes and stood there sky-clad…it felt very exhilarating..she dove into the cool water. It felt refreshing to her. As she swam a long snake snuck into the water. It swam silently toward her. As it was about to strike the Weeping Willow tree that had its branches nearly touching the water…suddenly came alive..it reached in and grabbed the snake and flung it far into the trees near by…they seemed to smack it down before it hit the ground.

Rosie looked up and said, " Thank you dear tree!" She got out of the water and went over and hugged the tree. It seemed delighted and yet embarrassed to have an angel wearing nothing but her birthday suit and hugging so dearly.

She quickly got dressed, eager to find Fabszy and tell him of this adventure she had endured.

When she found him he was staring at a wooden sign post. The writing on it said…" You have made it this far…straight ahead is the entrance to the cave of "OOG the Ogre".

Rosie quickly told Fabszy what had happened. He immediately embraced her…their wings then pushed them apart.

Fabszy said in a cheerful voice…``Nature and the birds and little animals have been so good to us..I think we should write a poem to them!"

Rosie quickly shook her head in agreement…as soon as she did the forest came alive..

Birds flew to them and landed on their lap and shoulders. Flower buds opened like a bevy of little ears bent to listen to their poems. The trees were gently rustling as in anticipation of the poems they would write to them.

Fabszy and Rosie took their golden quill pens from the nap sack and Rosie looked up with a grin and said you first...

Fabszy dipped his pen nib into the bottle of India ink and on a parchment scroll his poem -he did enroll....

The Right Path We Took

So mysterious is the choice to make.
The wrong one a vision can break.
To choose with just a flip of a coin;
The difference between winning or losing to join.

When the right choice is made
So much beauty comes to one's aid.
The vision of Nature's gifts unfold.
Serene gifts at times can be bold.

The waters of a babbling brook
Gave comfort to the Angel it took.
So wonderful is Nature's trust;
To make friends is a sacred must.

I look at my darling who shall be my wife.
I promise to keep her happy and free from strife.

We go now to meet our Fate
It lies beyond The Very Last Lost Castle
Gate…
(Fibby Bob Kinney (c)

The animal applauded, the trees swayed and
the flowers burst into bloom…

Fabszy looked at Rosie and said .."Now it's
your turn."

She smiled at him and turned to the animals,
birds and flowers and said.
"I love all of you very much…I will make a
poem for you..to keep you safe and free..and
you will know this poem is from me….

Ode to the Pristine Flowers

Dancing with the Breeze,
Putting all wildlife at ease
Even the melodious waterfalls
Kiss the radiant Sun rays that befall

Soulful eyes of water's tears
fill the wisdom of the laughing brook
Shy rabbits come out of their holes
Butterflies with tiny souls

Mother ducks bathing their chicks
Flirting bees flying from one flower to another.
That brings more life
To keep the forest free from strife.

Tiny fishes swimming in the river
Lily pads floating to deliver
The sound of water lapping the sand
Makes me feel happy and grand

The great old trees so deeply aged
With the wind and rain they are engaged
Vines hugging the wooden path lined posts
Green circling wood as its host.

Such beauty in this garden of green
To all a wonder to be seen
I, an Angel of the high order,
Send my love for you to discover…
(Fe Rosario V. Maximo (c)

The bird's chirped, the trees swayed, the
flowers burst into bloom. So beautiful was
Angel Rosie's poem.

Then, as if by magic they had passed another
test..this one to make Nature happy. As soon
as Rosie recited her poem aloud a new path

opened to them…they eagerly began their journey upon it.

Realm of Angels….Part 19
(The Ogre's Puzzles)

What a wonderful feeling it was to make Nature happy. Some had gotten this far only to forget about the beauty of Nature's gifts. They ended wandering around in a circle until they finally appreciated the great feeling that Nature provides when one is in tune with it. Only then was the path to go forward revealed to them.

Fabszy and Rosie found it very quickly as they were Nature lovers from the start.

Now this doorway was open to them. It was the middle path only visible when the riddles of the right and left paths were solved.

They walked hand in hand down the golden grass road.. the green grass had a gold tinge to the tip of each blade. It was like walking on a treasure of soft grass that led ever further up the mountain.

After they had walked about a mile they came to a wooden post. Upon it was a sign that read…"This is the entrance to the Ogre's lair. Let those who enter prepare to beware!"

Fabszy and Rosie looked at each other…then clasped their hands tighter as they walked into the dark cave opening. The golden path ended here as they passed through the opening of the cave.

As soon as they got inside..an iron gate closed down behind them. They were trapped. No way to go back ..only forward.

They walked cautiously into the dark damp cave. After they walked 20 steps a light emerged from the ceiling of the cave. They looked up and saw the cave's ceiling was open but full of bars. One could look through the bars but couldn't escape as they were tightly placed.

Although it was daylight when they entered, now the Moon was full. It shone its beams down to illuminate the two angels.

They looked ahead and saw there were three oak doors..each bore a sign upon it. The door to the left said…"Enter here and you will be cast outside..from there you must go all the way back and start your journey again."

The middle door said, " Congratulations, you have found the path to the Ogre's lair."

The third door said, " your choice is wrong..you are not worthy to go forward..you will be returned to the village where you must become one of the townspeople.

Fabszy looked at Rosie and said.."So that is why so many of the town folk seemed sad and unhappy…they must be the ones who failed this test!"
Rosie, nodded her approval..she added. " While I was at the boutique I noticed a sales girl crying softly. When I asked her what was the matter she blurted out…I used to be a princess, now I'm just a salesperson"
I see now why she was so upset.
Then she added…"If the doors are marked so specifically…then how do you choose the wrong one?"

They turned to look at the doors again and saw that the signs had reversed themselves. Now the door on the left said…"You have found the path to the Ogre's Lair"

They looked in shock and once again the signs changed … It was the revolving sign syndrome. The closer one got to the doors the faster the signs changed. To a point even when reaching the door with the right path..it changed before one could turn the handle.

Fabszy said I know the answer to this riddle. It is one I had worked on when I was a deep desire Angel. Just follow my lead.

He walked up to the middle door..the signs on it were flashing furiously. He stood with his back to the door. Rosie huddled next to him. He reached his hand behind him and grabbed the knob of the door…then he spoke these words aloud…

" The journey of a thousand miles begins with the first step…I take the first step backwards..and the journey is Over!!!"

He twisted the knob and he and Rosie were pulled through the door. When they turned around a sign said, "Congratulations, you have passed the test..the Ogre's Lair straight ahead.

Rosie was so happy..she reached up to give Fabszy a kiss.. but her protective dead wings pushed her back. Fabszy smiled at her and said.."One more to go -them we can see this Magic princess and find a solution to our problems.

They walked a few steps and entered a cavernous room. Standing there before them was a huge ogre.. about 8 feet tall and 500 pounds of muscle and tough hide skin. He stood there with his massive arms folded and smiled.

"Well, Well, look at these two fallen angels with broken wings. My predator pet bird has been following your progress. Very impressive I must say. If you are going to see the magic Princess you will have to get by me first."

Fabszy spoke up…"What is this test you will have us do?

OOG the Ogre spoke up.it's up to me to set the rules. In this case I shall be lenient in my puzzle..the test is you must make me happy. I assure you that is no easy task. However, I never get to see a beautiful fallen angel come here..so the test to pass through my door and meet the princess is I wish to kiss your toes.

Fabszy and Rosie looked at each other in shock..Fabszy spoke…"You wish to kiss my toes?"

OOG sneered…" Not you fallen angel guy….Her!"

Rosie was mortified…" You're a Toe Kisser!!"

OOG looked a little embarrassed…"Well, when you put it that way…under some circumstances…I am."

Before Rosie could speak Fabszy jumped in rage. He screamed as he brought his fist in direct contact with OOG nose. The blow started him… he staggered back a step and crashed on his rump to the floor. He looked up with a grin..wow, you angels carry quite a punch."

Then he got to his feet and said..I never fought an Angel bare knuckled before…but there is always a first time. Fabszy leaped into the air. This time his dead wings were on his side. They flared up over his head and smacked the startled ogre in his face. They kept beating on him…blow after blow trying to pulverize his puss into a mask of disheveled features.

OOG flexed the muscles on his massive arms and grabbed a wing in each hand. He whispered into Fabszy's ear…I could tear these right off your body…but I got a better idea. He twisted and bent the wings back at a very painful angle.
Fabszy screamed in pain.

Then the Ogre walked to the far wall. There was a large hammer and huge nails that lay on a table nearby.
He stretched Fabszy's semi-dead wings outward to almost their breaking point. He said with a sneer.
"This wall is usually for my trophies of the helmets and swords of the knights who think they can beat me in battle.

With you it's different. You are an Angel. I am going to nail your wings to the wall. I am going to crucify you."
He pinned Fabszy to the wall and reached for the hammer…when suddenly he heard a shout.

"STOP!!!"…he turned around and there was Rosie. She had taken off her riding boots and socks. She stood there barefoot before the Ogre. Her toes were painted bright red. She had done that for the wedding but never took off the Polish.

OOG dropped Fabszy in a heap on the floor and stared at Rosie.

The first words out of his mouth were…"Cherry Toes"…you have Cherry toes!!!"

Rosie smiled and said…"Yes I do" and I will let you give them one kiss in return for free passage to see the Princess."

OOG with a gigantic grin replied..consider it done..he walked over to her licking his lips.

Rosie said…"Wait…the agreement was for one kiss …and that's it!"

OOG said I never go back on my word..then he gently lifted her right foot and stuck the whole thing in his mouth.

Rosie Yelled…"I said one kiss…not a foot bath!!!"

And she yanked her foot out of his mouth.

He spoke with a sort of embarrassed look on his face…"Sorry, I just got carried away..I mean twinkle Cherry toes…ahh, wow!"

Rosie quickly put her socks and riding boots back on …she said with a grumble…"You got your kiss..now let us pass!"

The Ogre still smacking his lips said..I never promised We..I said I will open the door.. that was only for you…he stays with me as my trophy.

Both Angels looked up in disbelief. Rosie said with tears in her eyes.."I will not leave without him.

Fabszy finally got enough strength to sit up and say…"I am a poet… I will write a poem to you ..one that you can nail to your wall and keep forever.

OOG thought about it and said.."That does sound tempting..still I would rather have you nailed to the wall."

Then Rosie in her melodious voice sang the
words…"what if I wrote a poem to you too.
Then you could have poems from two angels
on your wall.

This perked the big Ogre up. He said..it's a
deal..write me a duet of poems and I will let
you pass the test..

Fabszy reached into his nap sack and took his
golden quill. Upon a parchment paper he
began to write his poem to OOG the Ogre.

A Second Chance

When is it a twist of fate;
As one stood near Heaven's Gate.
When the hands of time;
Reached down from the Sublime

So desperate was my cause.
To protect my dearest love because,
She was threatened by a devil's grip,
From her honor a vision did slip.

An Ogre of great power and strength,
Took from her a favor that went,
Into a trap that was my demise,

177

Yet, she saved me with her surprise.

So endearing was her quest;
To trick the Ogre with all his Zest.
He gave us his word;
To find the princess is our reward.

So dangerous is this beast with charm.
He promised freedom but delivered harm.
Only with the soundness of wit,
Can make this clumsy oaf sit.

He talked my poem upon his wall
Where valiant knights did fall.
(It isn't easy to pass the test.
Where strong men are lost to rest.)
My darling angel found a way,
To free me from bondage today.
Fibby Bob Kinney ©

Fabszy wrote the poem and handed it to the
Ogre. He read it with a furious look on his face.
Then he laughed out loud..."Fallen Angel I
must say you have a daring spirit in you. I
accept your insults...and modest praise... this
is a worthy poem. It will look good on my wall."

He turned to Rosie and said…"Let me see
what you can write to me." Then he added with
a grin…."Twinkle Cherry Toes"!

Rosie just glared at him and began her
poem….

"An Appeal to Ogre"
by Angel Rosie

Ogre of great strength and power,
You keep us your prisoners at this hour.
How much more do you want me to do?
To let us pass this crucial test by you?

I have done all you have asked
To make you happy; still you contest.
I obediently did what you wanted;
Now my dreams will be haunted.

Husband Fabszy tried to defend my honor,
Otherwise hitting you he would not bother
All he did was protect his dear promised wife
But you've tried to take his precious life.

Please stand back and let us pass
We need to see the Princess at last
She's the only one who can help our cause.
To lift the spell of fate and have it cast.

I ask you if you have an ounce of care
To let us pass; transgress we won't dare,
So our lives can finally become as one.
Two angels punished and thought done!

You scare people and consider it fun,
Yet deep inside you have compassion.
You may not be like any ordinary human;
Yet, you're intelligent to discern what's wrong.

Ogre, we humbly appeal to your big heart
Please do not keep Fabszy and I apart
We only wish to live in love and peace
Together freely to enjoy marital bliss.frVM
(Fe Rosario V. Maximo (c)

The Ogre read her poem and a tear came into
his massive eyes.
He looked at Rosie the Angel and said.."I never
thought of it like that. I only saw the dark side
to things. You have shown me that I do have a
place in my heart for forgiveness.Yes, you have
passed the test. Go and take your Angel
partner with you..you are free. The Princess
Brightly will help you now...tell her you were a
worthy couple to beat me at my own game..as I
am now a better ogre from the effort of your
victory..

Realm of Angels...part 20
(Meeting Princess Brightly)

The back door of the Ogre's lair opened.
Fabszy and Rosie stepped onto the golden
path that led to the massive gate that was the
entrance to the Very Last Lost Castle.

This path was not grass as were the others
that led the journey forward. This path was
made of bricks. Each one solid gold. Many a
King's fortunes are worth in these bricks alone.

When they got to the ivory gate they noticed it
was covered with diamonds. So dazzling were
these flawless diamonds that when the Sun
shone upon them they appeared to give a
rainbow of colors that bathed the walls of the
castle in brilliant colors.

The moment they arrived at the gate it opened
automatically.
The stepped inside and were greeted with a
bevy of cheers.

There in the silver circle were many elves and
fairies applauding them. The surrounding

stables were full of all sorts of animals living in harmony together.
From lions and tigers to turtles and rabbits each one as brothers and sisters to each other.

In the center of this magnificent circle was a marble fountain. It had many cherubs and winged animals spouting water in unison. The water was directed upward and fell back to the fountain base in a rainbow of colors.

The vision that impressed them the most was gathering at the golden steps that led to the castle. At first both Fabszy and Rosie thought they were a small herd of young ponies.

When they got closer they realized these were not ponies, but instead, they were Unicorns. And even more astounding was that some had two horns that came to a point..the fabled "Bicorn". Others had three horns that merged to a single point,
the "Tricorn" and most astounding of all the most magical horse of all.."The Quadicorn" the horse with four pointed horns on its head that formed a square. When it ran the horns would turn in a circle. They then would light up and sparkle with golden light. So magical was this

animal that it was never seen beyond "Uniland" the natural habitat of the unicorns.

So surprised was Fabszy and Rosie when the Quadicorn came trotting up to them with its horn blazing light. It gave each of them a nudge with its nose. They instantly began to glow in light.

They heard a voice..." That's enough Quadga let our guest relax.``

Both fallen angels turned to see the most beautiful princess they ever imagined to be.

She stood there in her gown of glowing light. Tiny stars were twinkling within it. She was a universe within herself. A flesh and blood cosmos of a living being. Upon her head was the ruby tiara of magical wonder. She held a star tipped wand in one hand and she raised the other in a greeting.

Let me introduce myself, she said with a musical voice..." I am Princess Ablaze Brightly...and I am here to grant your most fervent wish!"

The two fallen angels their mouths agape…Fabszy spoke first…"Dear Princess Brightly..our most fervent wish is to be married..our dead wings won't allow us to do that. They try to keep us apart."

Rosie spoke up…" We are from different kingdoms..I from the moderate desire..he from the deep erotic desire realm..together we have found a way to unite us both in a true loving relationship."

Princess Brightly looked at them and said…`` Your request is very challenging. I see in addition to your desire to be United your dead wings will not allow you to become close in desire with each other. This is a spell that goes all the way to the archangels of your two kingdoms. It is nearly impossible to be broken. Even with my supreme powers it will be difficult. However it can be done."

She touched her wand to the ruby tiara on her head and it began to glow. Then she said, "Fabszy and Rosie you will need more help to lift this spell. There are two others here who seek to earn their fervent wish.
Bobos the Jester…he wishes to become a master magician…Bami the Ogre's daughter

wishes to be respected for her true self and not looked down upon as a homely ogre with no talent to do anything on her own. Both these wishes seem that they can be overcome with just a flick of a magic wand. This is not true..as they are heartfelt wishes and must be earned. I can make treasures appear out of nowhere but heartfelt wishes must be earned.

She raised her wand and Bobos and Bami ran down the castle steps to join them.

All four joined hands ..Fabszy bonded with Bobos...and Rosie bonded with Bami.

The princess raised her wand above their heads and said..."From this moment on you will remember nothing of what I say...Fabszy I will make you a young handsome prince..and Bobos will be your wizard."

She turned the wand toward Rosie and said.."You will become a princess of breathtaking beauty..and Bami will be your best friend..who you confide with in all your major decisions. Here is the puzzle that must be solved. The spell to be accomplished is called "Pleasing the Princess ". Prince Fabszy will have to find a way to completely please

Rosie…this will not be easy…as both of you will still have your dead wings to contend with..although you will think they were imperfections you were born with and have to hide them from each other. Bobos will have to figure a way to help you..if you succeed he will get his wish also and become a master magician. Same with Bami when she helps Rosie to win..she will have the recognition she deserves. I wish you luck in this quest..as it is not certain that you will win..only with true ingenuity and determination will you reach your goal."

With that said, she twirled the Wand and her Tiara began to glow..in a flash all four of the wishful seekers were transported to a special realm within the castle grounds where their new journey was about to begin…

****

Realm of Angels…part 21
(The Tea Bag)

Supreme Princess Ablaze Brightly had transformed Fabszy and Rosie into a prince and princess. They had one major hurdle to overcome. Prince Fabszy had to find a way to completely please the princess..while still trying to hide and control his dead wings that would fight him all the way. Still he had Bobos the Jester to work with him. If this quest was a success then Bobos would become the master magician of his dreams.

Princess Rosie had her difficulties too. She had to fight her dead wings who were always trying to find a way to spoil her happiness. She and Mini the female ogre who has to overcome her own problems that are to be accepted for her true value ... together they must find a way to have Fabszy truly please Rosie.

Neither had a clue to their true identity..as this was part of the test. They must solve this problem on their own..only then-will they remember who they really are:

So their adventure begins
Prince Fabszy who was so very handsome that all the maidens in the land cheered just at the sight of him.

One exceptionally gorgeous princess whose name is Rosie took more than a liking for him. She sent a note by her favorite carrier pigeon that said, " if you can come to my castle tomorrow ...I will have pastry and tea with you".

The prince was infatuated with this decree. He had seen this princess as she lay sunning herself on the balcony window of her tower castle.

He decided to ride by on his magnificent golden palomino horse. She was sitting on a marble throne that was in the courtyard of her castle grounds.

He caught a glimpse of her as he rode, bareback, across the grassy knoll in front of the castle wall. At the top of the knoll gave him access to view the garden inside the gate that was the entrance to the castle.

In his light summer armor the Sun bounced off of him. It was as if his body was made of golden light as he glided effortlessly across the tall weaving grassy hill. Everything about him was perfect except for one thing. There was a bump on his back… and feathers could be seen slipping out of the back of the armor breastplate he wore. Nothing intrusive, just interesting to observe.
With the thumping of his horse's hoof beats the rider and animal came as one, it looked like a ghostly image gliding into view.

The princess Rosie sat on her throne with just a sheer gown that the Sun peeked through and nestled its warmth against her perfect body. Except for that slight bump on her back. So smooth and delightful were her curves that the Sun seemed to kiss every part of her.
She smiled and waved as the prince streaked by...then to even her chagrin, she shouted out, "Surprise Me!"

The prince heard her words as they were carried on a soft breeze. He made up his mind when he would visit her the next day for a chat and snack...there would be a special surprise for her.

As he returned to his castle he consulted with the resident jester/wizard...Bobos.
"What can I do to impress princess Rosie tomorrow at tea?"

The Wizard thought for a moment then responded with a smile on his magical face..."I think you should attend that afternoon tea event...as a Tea Bag!"

Prince Fabszy gave a laugh.. then he said to himself, "why not...what better way to get to know her than to have her drink me!"

He turned to the wizard and said, "tomorrow before tea time- you will turn me into a tea bag!"

The next day princess Rosie was sitting at the table in her castle garden. It was made of stone and the chairs were cast with precious stones embedded in them.
On the table were two beautiful Crystal cups and a golden teapot. There was an assortment of pastries and a basket of exotic tea to select as a choice.

As she was sitting there a pigeon flew to the table. It held a single tea bag in its beak and a note tied to its leg. The princess took the tea bag and placed it in her crafted tea cup. She took the note from the leg of the carrier pigeon and watched it fly away.

She opened the note and read it.
"My darling, dearest princess. I have come to you in the form of this tea bag.
Put me in your cup and pour hot water on me. Then I will become my most amorous. Let me warm up a little then put me to your lips. Taste me. Sip me. Let me savor the warmth and comfort of your perfect mouth. Then swallow me, slowly so I may feel the warmth of your

body as I am inside of you. Let me linger in your belly all day and night. Tomorrow, when I leave you...I shall evaporate in the air and become a prince again."

Princess Rosie was amazed by both the cleverness and the boldness of this prince. By tomorrow he would know her body so well, even better than she had ever known it herself. This embarrassed her a little but the thought of him being inside of her all day and night was too thrilling to refuse.

She decided she would write a note to him. She took her golden quill and dipped into the India dark blue ink..she wrote the note to him

("You Thrilled me quickly and surprised me!")

She read it quietly and tied it to the carrier pigeon's leg...it flew from her window on its way to Fabszy's castle. She said to herself.."let him read it when he gets home..he will know by then my body very well.. let my words thrill him even more when he reads my little note."

With that said, she went to the tea pot and poured a full cup of steaming water. Then she took the tea bag and caressed it in her long sweet fingers. She held it by the label and let it twirl in her hand before she dunked it into the hot water.

As she was ready to mate the bag with the simmering water she glanced at the label.."It said, "Ordinary Breakfast Tea"
She let out a shriek..."Oh No!!! I hate O.B.T.... I can't stand that bland flavor... Why is he not, Jasmine Pearl, or Jade Oolong, Guayusa, Rooibos, or even Darjeeling!!"
She took the tea bag and tossed it into the pond. A frog came by and quickly snatched it up and gobbled it down.

Bobos the jester/wizard had been watching this event through a telescope from Prince Fabszy's castle tower window. He sprang into action. He ran down the stars and jumped into a canoe that was in the waterway near the pond.
He quickly paddled his way down the stream and glided into the pond. There was the female frog bathing herself on top of a large lily pad.

He paddled up to her and said. " I saw you swallow that tea bag. I am here for you to cough it up right now. The Prince is in that tea bag!"

The female frog sat up on her hind legs and said…"Woa! You mean I swallowed a Prince? No way am I giving him up."

The Jester said…" I am his protector. Name your price. I will give you anything you ask if you burp up that tea bag for me!"

The frog thought for a moment and said.."Ok…I'll burp up the tea bag for one kiss..on the lips!" Then she closed her eyes and puckered up.

The jester said to himself.."sometimes we must make great sacrifices to save those we protect."
He closed his eyes and planted a big wet one on the frog's lips. The frog jumped for joy and spit out the tea bag.

The jester took it in the canoe and paddled back to the castle. He took the tea bag and in his wizard's hat he mumbled some magic words over it..the "Tea Bag" blossomed on the bench and in a puff of smoke the prince appeared in his own body.

He ran his fingers through his hair and said…"
You made me into a tea bag..but couldn't you
make me a flavor she liked!!!"

The jester bowed his head and said…"Sorry
Fabszy..but I paid a big price for my mistake..I
had to kiss a frog to set you free".

Then he found the note that Princess Rosie
had sent to him. He read it quickly and said,
"She is a clever princess…I must use my wits
to make her happy.

Prince Fabszy turned to Bobos, smiled and
replied.."we both learned a lesson here. I will
write a poem to the princess Rosie with my
apology..let's see if she will forgive me."

Fabszy took his golden quill and began to
write.

Forgive me once

Please dear princess of joy,
I come to you now as a boy.
One who made a terrible mistake.
As a Tea Bag that was not first rate.

I should have known you had fine taste;

Not to let that moment go to waste.
There is a reason that went amiss,
The better teas my Jester did dismiss.

He didn't have the keener taste;
That only comes when not in haste.
The finer teas take a while to brew;
But now he knows what to do.

Next time my choice will be more clear.
I will choose an object to bring you near.
Something that will make you smile;
So look for me in a little while…
Fibby Bob Kinney (c)

He put the poem in a pouch and attached it to
the carrier pigeon.
It flew directly into the tower window of the
Princess Rosie.
She read it and smiled….then she said…"I
wonder what form he will choose to try to
please me tomorrow? ….

Realm of Angels…Part 22
(Walk in My Shoes)

The next day the prince woke up with the realization that he had gone through one of the most devastating experiences in his entire life. Instead of being a cup of tea that the sweet princess drank now he was in a much different position. What would have been a wonderful experience…as a cup of tea to spend the entire night inside the warm belly of a beautiful princess.
Instead he found himself in the belly of a pond frog. Ugh, and who knows what else was down there with him. Not to mention the foul smell that engulfed him. He just couldn't wait for that frog to spit him out…as she didn't care for "Ordinary Breakfast Tea" either.

The jester wizard Bobos just shrugged off the prince's remarks then said, " your highness I think I have the answer to the problem. Write the princess a note and tell her how sorry you are for failing her expectations. Tell her you want to make up for it by transforming yourself into a beautiful pair of new shoes she can wear. Tell her this time you will make sure the shoes are from a well known designer and made with the finest quality possible.

The prince was happy with this idea and he sent the princess a note that he would arrive at her castle as a pair of slippers that she could wear with delight.

The next day as the Sun peeked its head over the tall trees of the forest all was set for this fairytale to come into bloom.

The princess awaited the arrival of the prince with excitement. She loved all her own shoes and sandals. The prince has promised her a new pair of designer slippers that she could wear to a lunch date with "Bami" the Ogre's daughter. Even though all the inhabitants in this kingdom shunned her. They thought she was beneath them. Yes, she was a bit heavy and her arms and legs were muscular...that was normal for a female Ogre...still the other princesses made fun of her behind her back. They would laugh and tease her when she walked by in a sheer gown. Her body was big but it carried her weight well. Her father was the most feared monarch in all the kingdoms. He was the one who held the post where the travelers had to pass his test and puzzles to reach the magic of Ablaze Brightly. Still, Princess Rosie, even though in a trance, she still liked Bami for what she was …and that is her good friend.

Then she returned her thoughts to the task to come.

It thrilled her that she would be walking on the prince himself. He would be beneath her feet the whole time at the luncheon. There would be music at her outdoor patio. A quartet of musicians. She would use Bami as a partner to dance with as the prince was already there inside her shoes. She would be careful not to step too hard on him. He would have to bear her weight all afternoon long. She would make sure to sit down once in a while. To take her weight off his back. She was worried a little if he could stand it when she stepped all over him. But then again, that's what he asked for... and she would give him his wish to be under her feet until lunch was done.

As she sat there pondering..a carriage pulled up at the front gate. A "foot-man" got out of the carriage carrying a velvet shoe box. He walked right up to the princess and presented her with the shoe box. There was a note attached to it. She grabbed the note and read it.

"My dearest princess, I have returned to you in the form of a pair of new lightweight slippers. My jester wizard put this spell on me and I will remain as your shoes until tomorrow at noon. Then I will turn back into my princely body and we may have lunch together for real. While I am to be your shoes there are a few requests I must ask you to make".

"First you must promise to step into me bare foot. I want to feel your bare feet stepping on me. Also, when you put your beautiful foot inside of me... please twinkle your toes. I want to feel your tiny toes tingle me with little kisses. As you walk on me I want to feel your toes touching me everywhere. I will be hugging the bottom of your feet as you walk on me. I will provide two straps that you can secure around your ankles. These are in essence, my very own arms. I will be hugging your ankles as you walk. Ok, now all that is left to do is pick me up in your sweet hands and strap me to your feet.. then walk all over me all afternoon long."

The princess was thrilled by the way the prince had conducted himself. He seemed to be a perfect gentleman. She would follow his instructions to the letter. She would be honored to step on him all day and night long!"

She carefully took the lid off of the velvet box. The silken slippers shimmered in the sunlight. They were the most beautiful shoes she had ever seen. They were made of a soft buttery material. Exquisite, yet simply in detail, and so perfect to look at.

She took them out of the box and put them on her lovely bare feet. She stood up in her new slippers and screamed...
"What the Heck is this? I wear a size 6 shoe and these things seem like they are a size 10…extra wide!"

She tried to take a few steps and the shoes flopped on her feet!
"These aren't slippers, she cried- they're flippers!"... I'm going dancing, not scuba diving!!!"

Meanwhile, the prince's face was not only getting stepped on.. but her toes were smacking him in the kisser. They were bouncing around in his ears or stuck up his nose as she tried to walk in these slippers. They were way too big for her. As much as she tried, all she could do was look like a bow legged bronco rider who was riding a wild horse.

She waddled over to the pond and kicked the slippers into the water. They floated helplessly on the surface. Some horney toads that were basking in the sun by the Lily pads sensed that this might be the prince they had been waiting for. They swam to the shoes begging for a kiss. The prince inside could only think of one thing, and that was ...."I have to tell the wizard that "One Size Fits All" doesn't work....and with that said he seriously thought about kissing a frog...until he realized the big one with his tongue sticking out was a Horny Toad.

At the last moment Bobos the Jester was paddling furiously in a canoe. He stopped paddling and cast in a fish net. The net grabbed the shoes a moment before the frog got his wish ..that is to kiss a prince..once again Fabszy escaped to try to please the princess again.

Once Bobos got back to the palace he put on his wizard cap and took the spell off of the prince.

Fabszy was furious.." How could I make such a mistake..I thought "One Size Fits All" meant it fit everybody. He turned to Bobos…"Why didn't you tell me that was just a general statement?"

Bobos gave a slight grin and said…"I have been wearing tousled velvet boots all my life..don't know much about shoe sizes"

Prince Fabszy said, " Now I have to write her a poem to tell her how sorry I am."

He took his golden Quill and began to write.

Shoes Aplenty

So sorry am I to say,
My jester went shopping yesterday.
He went into a large boutique,
One located at the end of Main Street.

He said, I want to but slippers as a surprise,
The salesperson said "What Size?"
He then replied, "I do not know..
Something that will fit her heel and toe."

The salesperson said " I have the very thing"
There is one shoe that you can bring;
It's the "One Size fits All,

To all feet it does call!"

So forgive this mistake
Tomorrow a new quest I partake.
I will think of something special for you
A new idea for sure brand new.
Fibby Bob Kinney (c)

Fabszy finished the poem and turned to the
wizard and said.
Tomorrow you will deliver me as a "Soap on a
Rope" when she bathes, tell her to make sure
she leaves a little of the bar of soap left on the
rope. Then she can give it to you and you can
bring it back here to the castle and turn it back
into me in my princely form..make sure you
bring that little piece of me back here so I can
become myself again."

Bobos nodded his head…"Don't worry I will
carry that little piece of you back here
myself..so nothing bad can happen to you."

Realm of Angels…Part 23
(Soap on a Rope)

"Soap on a Rope and Bath Water"

The wizard stood up and clapped his hands..."You have really done it...what a great idea! You can return to the princess in the form of a Designer bar of soap. One with a great lavender scent. It will be mild and creamy so it will be soft on her skin. The best thing is she will bathe with you. When she is in the bathtub you will be in there with her. She will rub you all over her body. She will love you as you make her so clean and smell so good."

The prince was delighted with this plan.
The next day a coachman knocked on the door of the castle. The princess opened the massive oak and iron door.
She took the package from the coachman.. he just stood there looking at her.
Then she remembered. It was a common practice to tip the delivery person when a package was delivered .
She sensed he was waiting for a tip. So she put all her effort into it and put a big smile on her face.
The coachman was so thrilled by her smile that he bowed and went happily on his way.

The princess thought to herself. One of the best perks on being beautiful is your smile is worth a small fortune. It can save you a lot of expense as you dish it out like candy when needed.

Then she opened the package and read the note attached to the bar of soap.
"My darling princess, I have come to you as this bar of soap. Please bathe in me. Let me cleanse every part of your precious body. I want to be everywhere on you. Nothing will embarrass or distress me from making you completely happy."

The princess smiled (this time no tip necessary).
She would bathe with the prince. They would do it all together and she knew they would find togetherness in this daring adventure. He will cleanse all the dirt off of me...Then she whispered to herself ...."I am not very dirty as dirt would not dare to cling to me...still it will be fun to see the prince lick up all the dirt he can find."

She let the bath water run hot in the large marble tub. It was giving off a little steam...but not too hot to sit in. She sat, full bodied in the tub. The bar of scented soap gripped in her long slender fingers...The silken rope around her slim neck. She began to rub her body with the soap.

The prince inside the soap could feel every curve of her perfect body. It was like he was in a sled on a snowy hilltop. Only, the snow was warm...and he floated over each hill and dale...he as the soap, and the princess body, as the environment.

Half way through the bath. The princess got carried away. The soap felt so good on her body she just couldn't get enough of it. She pushed it up under her arms...it felt so nice and the suds tickled her in the nooks and crannies of her womanly being.

The more she soaped herself the harder and faster she tried. The prince was aesthetic with joy. It was like being on a roller coaster...he was pushed and darted in a curving swirl of thrills... then he realized he was getting smaller. The princess had pushed him so hard and fast in and around her and never noticed he was melting.

Then in one final swirl and twist he was gone. The princess who had her eyes closed as she was dreaming in ecstasy.

Now, she opened her clenched hand and it was empty.

At first, she looked all around the sudsy bath water looking for it. "Did I drop him in my dream?" Then she realized she had used him up. She had melted him into nothingness. All because he made her feel so good.

She got out of the tub without saying a word. She toweled herself off and was reaching for the plug to let the dirty bath water go down the drain.

Just then there was a knock at the front door. The princess wrapped herself in the bath tower and went to the door. She said in a hushed voice, "who is it?"

A nervous voice came through the closed door.."did you pull the plug on the bathtub , yet?"

The princess gasped, "No, not Yet"

The other voice replied.."Good, that dirty bath water is all that is left of the prince..I am here to scoop it up and take him home."

The princess, still clutching the bath towel,
Took the rope from around her neck and
said…"This is all that is left of him."..She
blushed.

He carried an iron pail and went directly into
the bathroom. He scooped up the sudsy dirty
water into the pail and put the lid back on it. He
looked at the princess and said,

"That little ring around the tub is all that is left
of your bath. Wipe it down and all will be as
new again. I will take the prince home ..when
he recovers I'm sure he will pay you another
visit."

As the jester wizard was leaving he looked
back at the princess and said, "I trust your
bathing experience was enjoyable?"

She gave him one of her million dollar smiles,
and said..."it was great, but if I had to do it all
over again, I would prefer lilac to lavender."

The wizard thought for a moment and replied,
"it's always great when you can make a good
thing better!"…fBk

Realm of Angels....Part 24
(Black Forest Chocolate Cake)

The prince sat on his throne and contemplated his next move. He could still feel the bath water in his veins. It felt good because the princess had bathed in it. She nearly wiped him into oblivion as a bar of soap. It was so thrilling as she rubbed him, as that lather, all over her beautiful body. She literally melted him to nothing…but his memories of that bath were worth it.

He wanted to think of something that he could morph into where she could consume him totally. Well, maybe just leave a little bit of him to survive and cherish the experience.

Then the idea hit him. It was just like someone had hit him in the face with a velvet brick! "I got it!" He yelled out loud.."I will transform myself into a big hunk of Black Forest Chocolate Cake".

He looked over at his jester/wizard who was sitting at the table writing his memoirs …he yelled to him.."Hey Bobos" how do you like the idea of morphing me into a hunk of B.F. Chocolate Cake?"

The wizard looked at him and said, " There is not a girl in the world that wouldn't want to take a bite out of that tasty morsel!"

The prince got up off of his throne, He stripped down to his royal underwear. He had boxer shorts that were custom made in the "West Undies" they fit him like a glove (well, maybe more like a mitten) . .he stood on the kitchen table, his body strong and nimble, as he crouched himself into a tight sitting position.

The jester/wizard said a few magic words and the prince was transformed into a totally scrumptious hunk of chocolate cake. Actually it was more than that. All around the cake were strawberries lathered in whipped cream. On top of the cake was a delicious Maraschino Cherry. Yup, the princess was not only getting the cake she was getting the prince's cherry too!

The jester/wizard carefully put the cake in a box. He put a note in with it that said.

"To please you dear princess I offer myself as a piece of cake. I am here for your enjoyment and pleasure. After you eat me…please leave a few crumbs left. This way, my jester/wizard can make me whole again. I beg you…please leave a few crumbs of me so I can be a prince again. Your most loving admirer, " Fabszy Prince Pleasing".

The jester/wizard went to the princess castle. He put the cake box on the doorstep…rang the bell and ran away.

The princess answered the door and saw the cake box. She picked it up and took it to her dining table. She took off the ribbon (the prince was gift wrapped) and opened the cake box.

Inside she looked down at the most scrumptious hunk of cake she had ever seen. She reached down and picked up the princely piece of cake and laid him on an elegant plate. She took away the knife and fork. She would eat the cake with her bare hands.

So delicious it looked laying there, with strawberries and whipped cream oozing out of it. A delicate scent of honey filled her nostrils. She carefully picked up the cake in her two hands. She let it tease her taste buds. She was kissing it more than eating it. Then, the taste of the cake was so good..she grasped it in her fingers and stuffed it into her mouth.

Never, in her whole life had she tasted anything so delicious. The cake was tender, moist and incredibly scrumptious . She couldn't get enough of it. She gobbled the cake, while licking at the cherry at its peak.

Whipped cream was up her nose and got into her hair. She was relentless as she downed the princely piece of fabulously incredible chocolate cake.

Meanwhile, the prince, in the form of the cake, was in pastry heaven. Each bite tickled him to ecstasy. All he could do was to hang onto every sweet munch she took out of him. He was so pleased that he could make her so happy.

Finally, she was almost finished and she was licking her fingers. A few crumbs had fallen back onto the plate. She had remembered to do that. The prince, now reduced to a handful of crumbs, looked up from the plate and gave a weak, thank you. He was so glad for her sparing him. With these little bits and pieces he could redeem himself and become whole again.

A knock at the door. The princess yelled, " who is it?"
A voice came back, "I am the jester/wizard Bobos...I have come to take the crumbs, so I can take them back and make them into the prince again.

The princess got up from the table to answer the door. Above the table at the far wall was a bay window. It was open. Two female pigeons had been watching the cake ritual with great interest.

One female pigeon looked at the other and said...do crumbs from a princely cake sound to you?
The other one said, "They sound delicious "

Before the princess and the jester/wizard could get back from the front door, the two pigeons had flown to the plate and ate what was left of the prince.

The princess looked at the jester/wizard and said, "OMG the prince is gone! The pigeons have devoured him!
The jester/wizard just smiled and said…he is not gone…fate has reduced the prince to pigeon poop!"

He then gathered the two pigeons in a cage and took them back to his domain. The next morning when they did their duty..he gathered up the bird pellets and put them on the throne. He murmured a few magic words and the prince appeared.

He said, "how do you feel, your majesty?" The prince answered, "I feel like I'm made of pigeon poop!"

Then he slyly said, " but it was worth it, to please the princess!"
Now I have to think of what else I can do to make her happy!"

Meanwhile the two pigeons snuck from their cage and flew back to their roost. On the way back one pigeon looked at the other and said,``Do you think the gang will believe us when we tell them we pooped a prince?"

Meanwhile, back at the princess castle, just about the same time, the princess was thinking the same thing!…fBk
(Moral: "a craving for sweets can have its consequences!")

Realm of Angels….part 25
(The Paddle Ball)

The prince sat on his throne in deep thought. He was determined to find a way to truly please the princess. As he sat there slouched on the throne the Jester/ wizard entered the grand room. He was very excited as he approached the prince.

"Your majesty, I just came up with a brilliant idea. What if you transformed yourself into a paddle with a rubber ball attached to it."

He clasped his hands upon the tousled hat he wore upon his head then continued…"just think how much fun the princess will have using you as a paddle ball. You would be that rubber ball with a long elastic string attached to a wooden paddle. The princess could have a great time banging you all around!"

The prince jumped up off of this throne.. "Hey "Bobos!" That's a brilliant idea. I could be a little rubber ball that the princess could bang all over the place. She would love it. I would be a rubber ball in her hands. The more she banged me around...the more I could show my love for her. I would not complain as she bounced me off that wooden paddle. It would please me to know the more she whacked me around, I would never complain about it."

And so it became true. The jester/wizard cast a spell on the prince and turned him into a paddle with a little rubber ball attached to it.

The next morning a messenger delivered a package to the castle of the princess. The package was not sent first class, as the jester/wizard was very frugal when it came to spending money.
So the delivery guy just rang the bell and left the package on the doorstep.

This time the prince was incredibly lucky. Instead of the butler answering the door, as he would have put the package in the storage room thinking it was just junk mail, and forgetting all about it.

The princess herself this time was close by and she answered the bell. She opened the door and read the note that was on top of the package.

"Dear princess, it is I, the prince. I'm inside this box in the form of a paddle ball. You may play with me and bounce me around all day long. Tonight before the clock strikes midnight the Jester/Wizard will come by to pick me up and take me home. I hope you have a good time banging me around all day long. Your fervent admirer, the prince!"

The princess smiled and tucked the note into her breast pocket (actually there was no pocket there but you get the idea where she put it) she picked up the box and carried it to the kitchen table.
It had a blue ribbon and big brown bow that kept it secure. She took a pair of scissors and clipped them off. Inside the box was the paddle and ball as was promised.

The princess grasped the wooden handle of the paddle and began to flap the ball in the air....flap, flap, flap, ...she was having fun.

The prince who was inside the rubber ball felt every flap...to him it felt more like a slap. Gentle slaps that he could feel all over his body. It felt so good.

His voice almost like a soft whisper came drifting out of the rubber ball, " Go Ahead- Slap me harder, I love it!"

The princess swore she could hear the prince talking to her. She obeyed his command...she began to flap the ball harder...."flap-Flap-flapedy-flap"... now there was a rhythm going to it. Flappedy-flappedy-flappedy!!... The tempo was rising and the princess was getting into the pace and meter of banging this ball.

"Wham, wham, wham"... now she was really banging the ball!

The prince was in heaven. With each thrust he could feel himself hit the wooden paddle then rocket into space. The elastic tether would grab him at the height of the thrust and yank him back to the paddle...where he would bounce up off it again.

The princess was really getting into it now. She squatted down and grasped the paddle handle with both hands and began furiously slapping the ball…Wham-Bang- Wham- Bang- Wham-Bang!!!

The prince was getting plummeted…like he was riding a bucking bronco bareback…oh, how he loved every thrill of this ecstasy!

Then, on one extra hard Wham-Bang the elastic tether string broke and the prince, as the little rubber ball, went flying out of the open kitchen window.
He landed in the gutter and was immediately rolled down the drain pipe into the sewer below the castle. He lay there in the muck… which was extra mucky that day. To the horror and shock of the prince he had now become a "Slimeball" yes, the previously happy and contented prince was reduced to gutter trash…one minute he was a prince and now just a slimeball gutter trash rubber nothing. He cried, his life had gone to the depths from its lofty perch.

Water rushed by carrying the rubber ball into the river that flowed by the castle. A large big mouth bass saw the rubber ball. It looked like a worm that had rolled itself into a ball. The fish ate the rubber ball. The prince was now in the belly of the fish. This gave him hope as the fish could eventually spit him out and he would be free to roam the lake and maybe get washed up on shore.

At that moment some fishermen were fishing and one of them caught the big mouth bass. He took it to the dock and was cleaning the fish. When he opened it up he found the rubber ball. The prince tried to scream his plea…" I am not a rubber ball, I am a prince, take me to my castle and I will give you a king's reward for saving me!"

The fisherman actually heard the rubber ball talking to him. He held it in his hands and spoke directly to it.
"So you are a prince and you will make me rich by taking you to your castle!"
Let me tell you something, little rubber ball. If you really are a prince then take yourself home!
And he threw the ball over his head and laughed…then he said to himself…I have to stop drinking that fermented wine…or I may hear rubber balls talking to me."

In the meantime…the rubber ball sailed through the air and ended up going through the open window of an Italian restaurant… The stove was right near the window and a big pot of meatballs were simmering on the stove.

The princely rubber ball fell in with the meatballs. He was not only the same size as them but he looked just as delicious. Although the other meatballs couldn't talk they sensed something was different about this new meatball in their midst.
First of all there were no bumps on him. He was soooo smooth. He didn't smell like a meatball, no garlic on this guy. They became secret admirers of this really cool looking meatball. The prince sensed that he had a lot of new friendly meatballs as his pals.

Meanwhile, the jester/wizard went to the princess castle to collect the prince. She met him at the door and broke down in tears…"he's gone! The prince is gone- he flew out the window and I watched him go down the drain"

There was real concern in her tears as she cried upon Bobos shoulder. He spoke to her.

"It's not your fault. Come with me I will take you to have a meatball sandwich…that always makes me feel better.

The princess thought about big juicy meatballs, swimming in tomato sauce and dripping in garlic on a long hogie…the thought of it made her mouth water.

They went to the Italian restaurant down by the water. They both ordered meatball sandwiches with a little grated cheese on top.

When the prince felt the cheese sprinkled on him it tickled him a little. He watched from inside the bun as the waiter carried the sandwiches with two large soft drinks to the table where the princess and Bobos sat.

He looked up into the star filled sky as their table was near the bay window that gave an incredible view. The princely meatball looked up and said in a prayful tone …"please let her be the one who eats me!"

Yes, his playful plea was answered. The waiter handed the princely bun to the beaming princess. She took it in her soft beautiful hands…and rammed it into her mouth. She handled that hoagie like it was a battering ram…and her mouth was the gate to the fort.

She stuffed the whole end of that foot long princely bun into the depth of her full mouth. She bit down with her perfect ivory teeth and ripped a hunk of the sandwich (containing one total meatball, which was the prince) and that one bite filled her entire mouth. She tried to gulp it all down when she heard a tiny voice coming from the roof of her mouth.

The voice kept saying…"I wanted you to eat me…but I didn't mean Literally!!!!"

The princess reached into her mouth with two of her long fingers and plucked the prince out.

The jester/ reached over, took the prince, wrapped him in a napkin, and put him into his pocket.

He said, "let me take it from here"

He put the princess in a carriage and sent her home. It was now just past midnight. He walked with the princely meatball in his pocket all the way back to the Royal castle. He put the rubber ball on the throne..said a magic incarnation…poof!!! The prince appeared. The prince said, I still want to please the princess..but this time I must be something foolproof…

Realm of Angels- part 26
(The Silk Panties)

The prince sat on his throne in the royal study room. The jester/ wizard paced the floor in front of him. "Bobos" had come up with a lot of good ideas that had backfired on the prince. This time he was determined to change the prince into something the princess could truly be happy with.

It was like a lightning bolt went off in his head. He turned to the slouching prince and said…"I've got it! I will change you into a pair of frilly silk panties. The princess can put you on in the morning and wear you all day long!"

When the prince heard this he immediately straightened up in his seat. His body felt alive. His muscles quivered and his knees, which were bent now, shot straight up as he had been jolted into action.

He sat on his throne barefoot, he liked to do this when he was in a thinking mood. He twinkled his toes. They fluttered on his feet like a bevy of birds startled into a frenzy.

"That is such a wonderful idea" he muttered almost to himself. Then he added…."The princess can wake up in the morning and go take a hot bath. After she toweled off her warm body, now so fresh and clean…the first thing she will do is put on a pair of panties. That will be Me. I will be the soft silk panty that can cling to her curvy body. I will be part of the most intricate part of her. It will be me there to protect her and to keep her safe from all those nasty germs that try to creep up your legs when you aren't looking. They will not get past me. I will be her armor and shield in the form of silk frilly undies!"

Then he let out a "Yahooooo!" As this would be the perfect gift to please the princess.

The jester/wizard looked the prince straight in the eye and said…"we will have to be very discreet about this. The princess would be embarrassed if she knew you were a pair of panties hanging around her private parts. I suggest we go to the store that the fine ladies use to select their favorite underwear. It's a store called "Undies are Us" I looked into my crystal ball and found out the princess is partial to frilly silk undies. I will send her a note that says, " Special on sale today, "Plush Perfect Panties!"...she will run to the store to get this bargain. I will place you as the pink panty right on top of the stack of the "on sale" panties. This way, she can grab you, buy you, take you home, and put you on....taking a bath first, of course."

The prince was delighted by this vision of events. He stood up next to the throne and stripped down to his undies (this is important both for time travel- and panty transformation) . Now he sat bare boned upon his throne and "Bobos" the jester/wizard cast a spell upon him. A shimmering light appeared, then a rumble, before the prince tumbled, and turned into the cutest pink, silk panties imaginable. So soft and even the satin frills were warm to the touch. A pair of panties any girl in the world would be proud to wear. These were meant to grace the private curves of the princess...as they would please her as being precious.

Bobos sent a note to the princess telling her about the sale. The shop would open at 10 am that morning. Bobos got there just as the proprietor was opening the door. He went in pretending to be browsing around. When the shop owner wasn't looking he placed the prince in the form of the precious panties right on top of the "Special- on sale today" items. Then he left and stood in a doorway at the corner waiting for the princess to arrive.

The problem was the princess slept a little late that morning and she did not find the note till 10:30. Now she hurried to get dressed and ran to the shop to see what was on sale today.

Luckily the few women who had come to the sale had not seen the princely panties.. so far he was safe. Then, he felt a hand rummage through the sales bin and pick him up. At first, he felt rough fingers gripping him. He looked out through the frills and was shocked and horrified. The hand that held him belonged to an unmarried spinster. She was wrinkled with a bad disposition. She twirled the panties in her hand with a look on her face, "Should I buy these?"

First of all, the panties were way too small to fit her…she was an extra large..and these were a small (perfect princess size) …the Spinster thought for a long time then, she was disgusted with the thought that they could not fit her…and she tossed them back on the pile.

The prince was so relieved. At that instant the door opened and the princess walked in. She went to the sales bin and picked up the princely panties right away. She held the panties warmly in her soft hands and said in a whisper…"you are perfect. I will buy you and when I get home I will take a bath and put you on!"
The prince felt like he was in heaven when he heard those words"

The princess went to the register and said to the cashier, " I would like to buy these, please!"

Before the cashier could take her money a voice behind the princess said…"Excuse Me!"

When she turned around she stared right into the determined face of the spinster.

"You can't buy those panties as I saw them first. I put them down to look at something else but I had my attention on buying them."

At this moment the cashier spoke up. " That's right. I saw her holding those panties before you came into the store. I'm afraid she has first bid on them."

A tear came into the eyes of the princess. She dropped the panties on the counter and without saying a word she quietly left the store.

The prince was horrified. He tried to scream but the sound was muffled in the frills of the panties. The spinster paid for her prize and left the store with the prince now in a gift box..one that was meant for her use only. She muttered under her breath…I will make these panties fit me or stretch them beyond belief to do the job!

As soon as she got home she went to her bedroom and tossed the panties on the bed. Then she began to strip her clothes off. When it got down to her underwear she wasn't wearing panties…. She was wearing bloomers!

Then as in the immortal words of science fiction she recited…"I am going- where no man has gone before!"..

The spinster kept on her bloomers and stood in front of the full length mirror.

She reached over and picked up the princely panties and hammed her feet in them. She pulled and tugged at the panties but could not get them past her knobby knees. Finally in frustration she pulled them off and slingshot them out the open window.

They fell into a recycle bin on the corner. This is where people gave clothes to be recycled. At the recycling plant they had a store where some of the better stuff they found could be put on sale. Well, the princely panties were put on a mannequin and placed in the store window.

Yep, at that moment the princess who had been upset all morning because she had lost her opportunity to buy those panties that she fell in love with. She walked by the store and saw them on the dummy in the window. She bought them and took them home.

She said to herself…tomorrow when I wake up I will take my bath and put on my new panties. In a flash the prince thought about being next to her gorgeous body. There was a tear in his frilly eyes as he looked up into heaven above and said to himself…"all the pain and punishment I went through will be worth this one precious moment when heaven will open its gate to greet me."

The next morning , before the princess could bathe …a knock came at her door. It was the jester/wizard here to claim the prince. He told the princess what had happened and she was so delighted to know he had tried so hard to please her.

She held the soft panties in her hands and said…"Dear Prince I almost put to the precious part of me. That is reserved for my husband to be. If that will be you then you must please me completely first."

This brought a tear to the eye of Fabszy. He realized he had gone too far with his desire. He would have to find a way to please. He would try his best and never give up.

Bobos, then took the prince home in the hope to return again, in a new and different form…in his desire to make the princess happy …fBk

Realm of Angels.....part 27
(The Lazy Easy Chair)

It was once again time for the prince to try his best to please the princess. He had thought about it for a long time.
"What can I possibly change myself into that would give the princess great pleasure?"
Then he grinned to himself and said, "and of course, Me Too!"

He sat on his throne in deep thought. He was thinking how comfortable his throne chair was. It was made of soft leather and had golden lion heads on the arm rests.

He sprang up from his throne and yelled, " I've got it! I will change myself into a soft, easy chair so the princess can sit in comfort on me all day long!"

He called Bobos, the jester/wizard into the throne room. Bobos came in holding a catalog in his wizardry hands.
He joyfully spoke up, " Your Highness, I tuned into your thoughts and I like that idea very much. Here is the catalog of all the chairs and

loungers that are available today. Let us pick one you like and I will turn you into it.

The prince and wizard studied the catalog and the prince finally pointed to a page with a big comfortable leather chair..it was called, "The Lazy Easy Chair"..

"That's the One!" The prince yelled.." It's big, roomy and looks totally Comfy !!! Just like me. I will be that chair and the princess can sit on my lap. I can embrace her in my arms, which will be part of the chair. I can tickle her toes with part of me as the footrest! It's perfect. She will love sitting on me and I will embrace her body...the chair will be a recliner that can move up and down. She can even sleep on me. My Imitation leather will be buttery soft and totally huggable!"

So, Bobos changed the prince into the Lazy Easy Chair and it was delivered to the princess the next day. The note on the chair said. "My sweetest princess, I have come to you in the presence of this totally soft, supple chair. Please sit on me in comfort all day long. Midnight tonight my Wizard will come for me to take me home. In the meantime, please enjoy resting on my buttery laurels as you please."

The princess was overjoyed with how far the prince had gone to please her. She had two of the royal guards bring the chair into her sitting room. This is where she had her tea time and relaxed reading a good book. She went to her bedroom and put on a lovely silk gown. She wore nothing underneath it. Her body was so fresh and beautiful the silk clung to her curves as the light from the Sun shone through the big bay window. The golden rays of light seemed to kiss every part of the princess as she strode into the sitting room.

The soft comfortable leather chair sat in the room before her. It was so strong looking in its rich tan imitation leather.
The princess gave a little sigh then turned around and sat fully on the prince.

He gave a muffled moan as he felt the princess' firm body sit on his lap. It was one of the best feelings he ever had. Her body was strong and firm yet so light to the touch. She snuggled upon him and placed her long curvy arms on top of his smooth almost leather arms. He could feel her skin right through the flimsy thin silk robe she wore. He was in heaven and he wished she could sit on him, forever.

The princess sighed and said. " This is so wonderful I will go make myself some tea, "jasmine of course"… then I will come back and sit upon this magnificent chair…maybe even nap a little too"
She got up and scampered into the kitchen to make the tea.

The prince had reached a dilemma…should he keep to his word and stay in this position..or, should he change his mind and go for the ultimate pleasure.
If he reversed his position then his head would be on the seat cushion instead of on the headrest.

It was like a rabbit hole. Once you went down… there was no way to come back up. If he wiggled his body to change his position to facing down… that is where he must stay.

The prince thought about it and said to himself. " I know it's wrong to go for something selfish. I would only be getting pleasure out of it and it's not the right thing to do. I can't help it. The thought of being that close with the princess is worth the risk."

The prince wiggled himself inside the leather looking lounger so his face was now on the cushion and his legs were where the lounger arms should be. His hands were down by the footrest. He could tickle the princess' toes with his fingers when she sat down.

Just then, the princess came back into the sitting room. She had a hot cup of tea in her hands. She put it down on the coffee table and touched the arms of the longing leather looking lounger with both her hands. She was ready to sit down when a knock came upon the castle door.

She stood up straight and said, " Who is it?" A voice on the other side of the door replied, "It's me Barni, the Ogre! Remember, last week you invited me to come over and have tea with you today!"

The princess with a startled look on her face, responded…"OMG Bami, I forgot all about our tea date. Please come in the door is open"

The castle door opened and there stood the ogre's daughter. She was considered cute and remarkably agile for an ogre.

Her dad was the mean and nasty Ogre OOG. When it came to his daughter he gave her anything she wanted. The time she made friends with the princess meant her castle was off limits to all the bad animals in the forest.

Incredibly, Bami was wearing the same type of silk robe, with nothing underneath it...just like the princess.

Bami, limbered into the sitting room. The first thing she said, " Oh, what a lovely longing lazy lounger...it looks so comfortable, is it new?.

The princess sighed and said, "Well, kind of...I am just borrowing it for a day."
"Why don't you make yourself at home... I will go make you a cup of tea..." she gestured for Bami to sit on the couch on the other side of the coffee table. Then she went to make her some tea.

Bami started for the couch then half way there she changed her mind. She said to herself... maybe I will go see how comfortable that lazy longing leather looking lounger is!"

The prince sensed this and said , "Oh No, that ogre is coming over to sit on my face. With a buttocks the size of a prize winning pumpkin...I am doomed.

With that said, Bami came over and sat right on the prince's face ...squashing him down like a pancake.

When the princess returned with the tea she was shocked to see Bami sitting there with a big grin on her face.
The princess sat in her regular chair and of course, Bami wasn't budging off her new found favorite "Lazy Longing Leaning Leather Chair"

They chatted all day long and at sundown...Bobos sensed something was wrong and he sent a carriage to pick up the Last Lazy Longing Chair.

When he got it back to the castle he changed the prince back into his normal self...although, his nose seemed a little flatter.

The wizard said to the prince, "What have you learned from this experience ?"

The prince then tweeted his nose and said, " if you are going to change your point of view..then you better be prepared for the consequences!"…fBk

Realm of Angels …part 28
(The Magic Pen and Ink)

The prince was really distraught. It seemed everything he tried to do to please the princess had backfired on him. As hard as he tried to please her it just didn't work well. His good intentions came back to haunt him.

He sat upon his throne in deep thought. Bobos, the jester/wizard, entered the throne room. He had a paper and pen in his hand. He spoke in an excited tone.

" Your Highness, I am getting ready to make a list of the things you would like me to turn you into so the princess can be pleased with the results!"

As he was speaking a really bright idea lit up in the prince's fertile mind.

"I've got it, this time I really have a wonderful way to please the princess!
I will have you turn me into a fountain pen. This way, the princess can grasp me in her long soft fingers and write on me all day long. I will become the words in her mind. As she clutches me in her hand I will become the words she writes, mingled with my own. We will be one together...pen and writer in a bonded grasp!"

Bobos the wizard applauded. " That is a great idea, your Highness. I will change you into a beautifully crafted fountain pen."

And so it happened. The next day came a rap on the princess castle door. She opened it and a messenger handed her a velvet laden box with a note attached to it. She took the box inside and sat it down on the desk in her writing room. She opened the note and read it aloud.

"My dearest princess, I have come to you in the form of a magic pen . Please write all the wonderful words in your heart as you hold me tightly in your creative fingers."

The princess put down the note and gave a little laugh…she spoke up, "how clever is this prince. He is so dashing and charming! I will hold him in my fingers and write with him all day and night long."

She opened the velvety box. Inside was the magic pen and a crystal bottle of dark ink. She would fill the fountain pen with this ebony ink and begin writing her fondest memories.

She dipped the pen nub into the ink and filled it full of the shimmering dark ink. She took her diary out of the protective mothballs. She had a diary but never used it because she wanted something special to happen before she wrote her first words in it...this was that special moment and now she was ready to pour her heart out in words that would last forever.

With the magic pen in her hand she sat at the writing desk. She dipped the nub into the ink and filled the body of the pen full with the glowing dark ink.

The prince felt the depth and the warmth of the ink as it filled him full. It was like blood that flowed in his veins. He felt the body of the pen as his own. The silvery tip point was his brain. As the princess transferred her thoughts to the bonded paper he would mingle his own deep words within them. Together they would write a masterpiece. It would be all about the deep emotions they felt for each other.

The princess opened her secret diary. She was ready to put her innermost thoughts down upon the cream colored paper that filled the bulk of the red leather diary. She held the princely pen in her fingers and pressed the nub upon the gilded page. Together, they began to write.

The words in carefully crafted sentences began to cascade from her mind. It was like a grand symphony orchestra pouring forth a concerto of carefully crafted imagery. So beautiful were her sentences that they flowed effortlessly into paragraphs that began in poetry.

All day and into the night the princess wrote at a furious pace. Finally, it was done. Together they wrote a bevy of poems that would last a lifetime. The diary was full to capacity.
The princess took a cool drink of her choosing and then went to her carriage.

It was still early evening. She would take a ride over to her best friend's house..that of Bami the Ogre. There, with Bamii and her dad, OOG The big bad ogre (who was friendly to her

because she was his daughter's best friend).
The princess thought they would be the perfect
audience to judge her fine work.

At the Ogre's den, Bami and daddy ogre sat in
anticipation of the words written in the princess
diary.
The happy princess stood there, in the massive
sitting room of the Ogre OOG's dungeon
castle. She opened the diary and was ready to
read the treasured words contained inside.

Instead of reading , she screamed. She
screamed so loud it nearly broke the crystal
glasses that Bami and Her ogre daddy were
drinking droolnip (ogres favorite drink) from!
The princess screamed again then shouted out
loud…"it's blank- where have all the words
gone??? The entire diary is Blank!!!"

The prince inside the pen then said to
himself…"Oh, No, when Bobos told me to go to
his "Cabinet of Tricks" and pick out an ink that I
liked…I must have chosen the
"invisible"ink…the one that looks real then
after a few hours all that is written with it,
disappears! Why didn't I read the label,
instead I just went for the bright alluring color
that it showed on the bottle..I made the

princess lose all those beautiful words we wrote together…I am doomed because of my bad judgment."

With that said, in his pen mind, the prince collapsed.
The princess dashed to her carriage and cried all the way back to her castle.
As soon as she got there her fury drove her to the supply closet where she kept her arts and crafts supplies. She tossed the princely pen into a box with a lot of junk and unused craft tools in it.
There were Crayons, Marker pens, broken pencils, chalk and erasers, and even so called Magic markers, and also, the lowly rubber erasers.

The princely pen bounced in the bin…Immediately, all the other supplies started to make fun of him.
"Look what we got here!" A bottle of "white out" said, " I thought I was a bad boy by blotting out all those mistakes. This guy did it on purpose… he is a real loser."

The supplies didn't show him any mercy.
The kiddie crayons began drawing pictures , then smudged all over them.

The blackboard chalk mocked him, "ha ha, we can do what you can't do!"
The permanent markers gloated, " you could never be as good as us...we are forever!!!"
Even the erasers taunted him.."We like you because you don't make us work. We can relax and let you do all the erasing for us!" This caused some big guffaws among the artists brushes as they knew what it felt like to be wiped clean by turpentine.

The next day the wizard came to get the prince. The princess told him what had happened. Bobos, slapped his hand on his four pointed jester's hat and said, "That explains it. I went to get my invisible ink this morning and couldn't find it!"

This caused the princess to smile for the first time. She said, " I guess that invisible ink was just doing its job. We can't blame it for that."

Then she added, "If we all did what we were supposed to do...it would be a better and wiser world we live in."

She then went to the storage bin and retrieved the princely pen. She was about to hand it to the wizard when she stopped and brought it up

to her lips. With a happy tear in her eye these words left her lips…" you have tried so hard to please me. I thank you dearly, and I will give you one more chance to make it right."
With that said she put a kiss on the pen and handed it to the wizard. He bowed and took the pen back to the royal castle.

After the pen was returned to the image of the prince. He sat there, on his throne and said to the jester/wizard .
"The princess has granted me one more time to please her. I will not waste it. This is my opportunity to show my true feelings for her. I will write all this as a "Letter".. you, my faithful Bobos will deliver the letter to her…and we shall see what Fate has in store for us…fBk

Realm of Angels…..Part 29
(The Letter)

To my only love;
I write this letter to you before I go upon the journey to reach the peak of the mountain. I want you to know this, to read my words, as the journey is an impossible task that must be done. If I do not return then let this letter be the hero you hold in your arms. As it will become the whole of me:

You are so beautiful when you gaze upon your
own face the light about you trembles in the
mirror.

Your eyes are bright sapphire blue,
as if carved from the most translucent stone,

The lashes of your eyes, like little hands,
Ever stretching upwards as if to reach the
heavens,

Then bowing in obedience with
Every time you blink them.

Your brows, the loveliest, softest curls of
golden brown,
Resting upon your lids in living color, hues of
pink.
To embrace the azure of the blue in view,
Is to see the rainbow innocence of your face.

Your forehead, smooth as fine silk in texture,
Radiant in color and its sheen unlined and
pure.
I compare you with pleasure true
To the rarest pale gemstone.

Your hair, grows from your head like a wild
garden;
Exotic tall grass carefully cultivated and
managed
Strands of yellow gold,
With hints of wild flowers at every braid.

Below your eyes, the magnificent edifice of
your nose.
So terrific is your nose, if your face were a
church,
It would be the crown steeple,
True at no matter what angle it was observed.

Your Ears, sea shells, Mother of Pearl,
Caressed by the golden wings of your hair.
Your Hairline, bathed brightly by the Sun's
rays,
That shimmered at every turn of your head.

Your Cheeks, obediently gleaming upon your
face.
Twin mounds of glistening life nestled soft and
smooth.
The perfectly balanced landscape of your
features
A music box magistracy in tune with your
smile.

Your Chin, like a peach with the fuzz of youth,
Delectable, ripe, and unpicked.
Your lips, a flower blooming upon your mouth
The pedals flutter and your unspoken words
thrill me.

Your face goes into celebration with each new
word.
Your eyes dance, your brows applaud,

For the words you speak are born to win
Everything at their chance to play.

You are the Angel face of my love,
The way I seen it each morning

As it brings me out of the darkness of sleep,
Into the longing Light of the living day....
Wait for me, please, and with my return, in
flesh and blood...or just in the reading of these
words, for we shall covet together our first kiss,
as much as we shall cherished our last...fBk

The prince with tears in his eyes put the letter
in an ivory envelope. The words were hand
written in a golden tinged ink. The entire poem
glowed upon the hand bound paper that held it.
The prince placed the letter inside the

envelope and let his tears fall upon the glue that closed the flap on the envelope.

He hand wrote the princess address and went outside the castle. A mailbox was next to the large elm tree. He placed the envelope in the mailbox and watched as its metal lid closed shut.

Then he went back to his castle and without another word said. He dressed and left a note for his wizard Bobos. It simply said, "I'll be back, maybe?" Then he left.

The next day when the mailman opened the mailbox he noticed the letter from the prince. He picked it up and examined it closely. Then he took a pen from his pocket and wrote on the envelope, in the space where the stamp was supposed to go…"postage required " he then went over to the castle and dumped the letter at the prince's door step.

Prince Fabszy had managed to climb the steep trail and went through the trap set to stop anyone from reaching the Lost Castle. He figured out the way through sheer determination. Now he was at the castle gate. Battered and torn he saw the Supreme Princess Ablaze Brightly sitting upon a stone chair in the garden. He approached her cautiously.

He spoke with a heaviness in his heart. "Dearest Brighly. I tried so very hard to do my best to please Princess Rosie. Everything I did failed. I thought my letter to her would show my true love and she would finally be pleased. As I was ascending the last barricade to your palace I remembered I forgot to put a stamp on the letter I sent to her. She will not receive it…my love is doomed. I would give anything for her…I am offering my life to save her. Take me and let the Ogre have me as his trophy. All I ask is you give Rosie a life without her dead wings."

He knelt and bowed to Princess Ablaze Brightly.

She rose up from the stone chair and approached Fabszy. At that moment a carrier pigeon flew to her shoulder….it was carrying a letter in its beak. She handed the letter to Prince Fabszy and said… "This is the letter you had sent to her . Take it now in person. You have passed the test. Your love is stronger than the spell that binds you."

With those words Fabszy's dead wings rolled off of his back and fell to the ground. He was free of the spell that had haunted him for so long.

The Supreme princess smiled…. "Yes, you are still an angel.. but your wings are now invisible. You can fly as much as you like in your dreams. Go now as soon as Rosie reads your letter she will be free from her spell.Then come to me and I will personally grant you marriage."

In a moment of total joy Fabszy almost flew all the way back to his kingdom. He ran over to Rosie's castle. She was sunning herself on the patio in her garden. When she saw him she jumped to her feet.

He ran up to her and said… I wrote this letter to you…. please read it aloud now. She immediately opened the envelope and began to read the letter aloud…Half way through it tears of joy flooded her eyes…as they did her dead wings fell off of her back. She read the last few lines with a smile and love in her voice.

She Turned to Fabszy with her face in bloom and said… "Yes, oh Yes, I will marry you and give you a child to bear your name and someday find greatness."

They kissed longingly…with no dead wings to keep them apart.

Realm of Angels…..Part 30
(The Conclusion)

Fabszy and Rosie now without their dead wings to keep them apart could embrace each other freely. Still, Rosie would stop Fabszy and say…. " We can't go too far till we are married. This made Fabszy work harder to traverse the terrain and get back to the Very Last Lost Castle.

Finally, their efforts were rewarded. They, with Bobos and Bami in tow, made it to the front gate of the palace.

The supreme princess was there waiting for them.The huge gate opened and they entered the garden. It was filled with flowers in bloom. Butterflies danced in a parade of fluttering wings as the petals on the flowers applauded.Bees buzzed with the thrill of nectar in their bellies. Trees swayed..and the weeping

Willows with tears of joy on every green leaf
that fluttered in the warm breeze.

The four of them entered the castle
grounds..the great gate closed behind them.
The glowing brightly princess, her Ruby Tiara
ablaze with eternal light as she spoke
softly.."You all have done well..and your
rewards well earned."

They bowed to her …waiting for the thing they
cherished most.

She called Bobos…he walked up to her and
bowed his head. She smiled and said …"You
dear jester have passed the test. It was your
ingenuity that rescued the prince from his dire
predicaments." She touched the glowing
Emerald stone on her Tiara and an oak bench
with a sword, cup, wand, and coin appeared.

She pointed and said…"Go to the bench and
claim your tools…as you are now the rank
of…"Master Magician"

As soon as he touched the tools his Jester's
cap was turned into the invisible hood and
cape of magic wonder. He stood there proudly
as Master Magician.

Princess Ablaze turned to Bami the Ogre's daughter...she stood and came forward.

The Supreme Princess touched her Tiara...a bolt of light shot out and covered Bami in its glow...Ablaze Brightly then said.." From this moment on no one will ever laugh at you or speak behind your back. You will carry yourself with the presence of a princess. Friends will seek your advice and enjoy your stories of what you have seen in the kingdoms you have had the good fortune to travel to and return safely. You now have the power to convince your demanding father to be more lenient when they encounter his puzzles to pass to see me!"

Bami was overjoyed. She said heartily..."Thank you dear Supreme Princess...you mean my Dad will finally listen to me..and accept my requests..that is totally Awesome!!"

She scampered off in a hurry to put her father to the test of her demands; for once.

Ablaze Brightly turned to Fabszy and Rosie...she bade them to come nearer to her.

They came close arm in arm. The Supreme Princess spoke clearly and directly to them.

"I am very impressed with how you handled all the problems and trials that were cast upon you. Your dead wings are gone...but the invisible ones will last forever. You can fly wherever you please in your dreams. Your greatest wish is to be married. I will do that for you now."

As soon as she said that Fabszy reached inside his tunic and pulled the chain he wore around his neck. At the base of the chain was the wedding ring he had gotten for Rosie back at the Swann Lodge. He said to the Supreme Princess. I have kept this all this time in hope of one day putting it on Rosie's finger."

Ablaze said ..."Then put it on now...as the power within me as Supreme Princess...I now pronounce you Husband and Wife...you may kiss the bride."

With the ring firmly on her finger...Rosie turned and found herself in Fabszy's arms. He said softly, " We are married now...let this as our wedding kiss..be as warm and wonderful as our life together."

They embraced in a deep loving kiss that was the reward for the trials it took to get here, in triumph now.

They turned to look at Princess Brightly…she was waiting for this moment… to direct their lives to where they would be going forward.

She pointed and spoke…" You will take that new path. The one with the glowing golden light. Follow it through the thick trees and it will lead to a small village. Behind the village there is a log cabin with a woodsman and his wife. He was a great knight in his early days. She is a princess of a very high order. They too have passed their trials and ordeals. You will find a cottage next to theirs. The four of you will be best friends…they have a daughter and you shall have a son. Your children will be real angels. Your son will be as Cupid.
And the daughter will be as Eros
You may name them…Cupidda and Erosaa

They can fly freely and shoot arrows from their magic bows. They will have the power to stop quarrels between lovers…and bring love to those who seek it. Go now and fill your duty to Fate's call.

Fabszy and Rosie walked the long golden path to the small village. They were welcomed warmly by the Villagers and small animals that were friendly to all.

Sure enough there was a cottage waiting for them. And they and Fabbo and Anneto became best friends...their children Cuppida and Erosaa, were a real team of loving angels...both as children and the love they brought to others in need.

Is this the end of this Angel-tale or just the beginning of the adventures of Cuppida and Erosaa? "The angels of loving grace"...that awaits in another Angel-tale to be told...fBk

Thank you dear readers for taking this trip to the "Very Last Lost Castle"...that is the title of my other book that gave me the idea for this sequel.
I am so thankful to "Fe" .... Who is the inspiration for Angel Rosie..."Fe" lives in the Philippines and is the mother of three children..with six grandchildren. I met her through the many poetry forums we are both involved with. It started with her writing a poem. I found that poem very enjoyable and I

wrote a follow up poem to go with it. That led to a collaboration. We did many collaborations together. Some appear in this book. She is a master at writing poetry as many of her poems appear in this book.

On the next few pages there are awards that we received over the past year...there are many more that we both have but those would make a book by itself.

Look in the future for more Angel-tales...by the Angel-tale teller....Fibby Bob Kinney.

The next pages contain some of the awards we received for our poetry. I also have 16 books in print...ranging from fairytales to poems..and a semi-autobiography called, "Thoughtful Dribble.

Fe Rosario V. Maximo (Fe)

Fe Rosario V. Maximo taught Advanced English Grammar and Advanced Composition . She was schooled at the University of the Philippines , Philippine Christian College , and Cagayan Teachers College. She graduated from college with the degree of Bachelor of Arts , major in English and minor in Psychology.

She lives in Paranaque, Philippines with three children and six grandchildren.

You can email her at: fvmaximo43@gmail.com

THE TEMPLE OF IMPECCABLE WRITERS

CERTIFICATE
OF EXCELLENCE

Proudly presented to:

Fe Rosario Vergara-Maximo

In recognition of his/her contribution to the Arts Of Literature for inking a brilliant Quote about Christmas, given by the TTIW platform.

WINNER

Given this 29th day of December 2022

CHUKWUMA CHIKA OGBUEFI
Founder/President

Organized by:

GLOBAL POETIC PEN

A Brawny Dreamland of Poetry

Poet Of The Day

This certificate is proudly awarded to

Fe Rosario Vergara-Maximo

At The Threshold Of My Heart

(Poem)

For your invaluable contribution
and generous support by sharing
your brilliant composition to GPP

ADMINISTRATIVE TEAM
Jun Valerio Bernardo
Amb Maid Corbic
Mon Maya Mongar
Deepti Shakya
Sarita Poudel
Marisan Ortiz
Auwal Sulaiman Burji
Sangay Lhamo
Ahmed Murphy Dorley

Mohammed Hamim
(Founder & CEO)

Deepti's Design

Issued on:
June 5, 2022

262

Fe Rogario Vergara Maximo

Star poet of
Rhythm of Arts
June 2022

Founder
Bibhudutta

Admin
Bijayalaxmi

Sparkling Quill

Awarded Certificate

of

Gold

METAMORPHOSIS

Fe
Vergara
Maximo

AUGUST Monday

Sabrina Sewpath
Founder
Vee Maistry
Co founder

22/06/22

Rupali Gore
Executive director
Roebain
Administrator

264

UNITED POETS @ HEART

SPECIAL AWARD

SPOTTED ARTIST OF THE DAY
EDITOR'S CHOICE

This award is proudly presented to

Fe Rosario Vergara Maximo

Title: WHY I CHOSE YOU
Given this 24th Day of April 2022

fo rose

ADMINS
Gly M. Andrade
Asha Kumari
Marisan Ortiz
David Soh
Onyinyechi Cosmos Etu
Mr Abdur Rashid Miah
Rohit Sharma

Veronica R. Pingol
UPAH FOUNDER

265

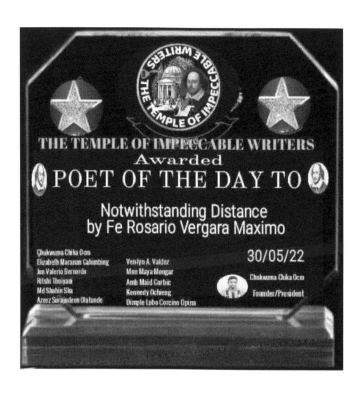

THE TEMPLE OF IMPECCABLE WRITERS
Awarded
POET OF THE DAY TO

Notwithstanding Distance
by Fe Rosario Vergara Maximo

Chukwuma Chika Ocm
Elizabeth Maranan Cabimbing   Ven-lyn A. Valdez   30/05/22
Jun Valerio Bernardo   Mon Maya Mongar
Ritshi Thoiyam   Amb Maid Corbic
Md Shahin Sha   Kennedy Ocheeng   Chukwuma Chika Ocm
Azeez Surajudeen Olatunde   Dimple Lobo Corcino Opina Founder/President

266

OXYGEN PEN

6/5/2022

STAR POET /POETESS of the day

CERTIFICATE OF EXCELLENCE
FOR OUTSTANDING WRITE
PRESENTED TO

FE Rosario Vergara Maximo - Soul Mates Forever

Sulagna Mitra
General Secretary

Gayan Hettiarachchi
Director

Reshma Sabrina Sampath
GM/Chief Administrator

267

CHAUCER'S SQUARE

MONTHLY REVIEW

June 2022

Poet : Fe Rosario Vergara Maximo (Philippines)

Poem : In Our Own Time And Space

Reviewer : **Ankita Baheti (Qatar)**

Best Wishes
To the poet and the reviewer

Poet Of The Day

This certificate is proudly awarded to

Fe Rosario Vergara-Maximo

The Woman And Her Reflection

(Poem Title)

Four your invaluable contribution
and generous support by sharing
your brilliant composition to GPP

Issued on: *May 18. 2022*

Mohammed Hamim
(Founder & CEO)

GLOBAL POETIC PEN

Poetic Hearts
MOVING TO A NEW HORIZON

Year End **CERTIFICATE OF RECOGNITION**

is presented to

Fe Rosario Maximo

Special Awardee for introducing the new verse of collaboration in her unique poetry form.

."Given this 25th day of December, 2022.

PH Founder

PH Consultant

Fe Rosario Vergara Maximo

Star poet of Eternal Flames

14/11/2022

SPARKLING QUILL

Education is Indoctrination

POET/POETESS of the day

Certificate of
Excellence presented to

Fibby Bob Kinney / FE Rosario Vergara-Maximo Realm of Angels part 3

Reviewed and Selected by

Sabrina Sewpath

SABRINA SEWPATH – FOUNDER
ROEBAIN CHRISTIANS – EXECUTIVE ADMINISTRATOR
DIVYA KAPOOR GOSAIN – CHIEF RECITALS MANAGER
BHAKTI GALA – GENERAL SECRETARY

THEME : "On Passion and Purity"
10th Poetry Collaboration of
Fibby Bob Kinney
    and
Fe Rosario V. Maximo

(**To...** See more

SPARKLING QUILL
Special Mention
Madhatter Tuesday with Vee

8/2/2022

Certificate of excellence in humour presented to

Fibby Bob Kinney

Rupali Gore
Chief Admin

Tee Murugi
Admin

Sabrina Sewpath
Founder

Vee Maistry
Co-founder

Sparkling Quill
Certificate of merit

PLATINUM   Admin Team:

Reshma Sabira Sownath
Vee Maistry
Rinali Gove
Reebain Christians

Fibby Bob Kinney

Mad Hatter

1/3/2020

Poet of the Month
November 2022
The Brook Song International

Certificate of Participation

Hind Desh Parivaar

Date: 26-11-2022

ISBN 97893991358921

International Literary Award

Proudly presented to

Fibby Bob Kinney

For being a co-author of International Anthology

'Amar Vishv Sahitya'.

(World Literature Forever)

Best Wishes for your bright future.

UNITED POETS @ HEART

CERTIFICATE

OF SILVER AWARD

This certificate a proudly awarded to

Fibby Bob Kinney

SUNDAY CHALLENGE
Theme: WISH
Date Published: May 23, 2022
Given this 28 Day of May 2022

Signed:

Veronica R. Pingol
UPAH FOUNDER

www.motivationalstrips.com

MOTIVATIONAL STRIPS™
World's Most Active Writers Forum

Rabindranath Tagore Memorial
Certificate Of Literary Appreciation
Presented To

Fibby Bob Kinney

For His / Her Literary Contributions Equalling World Literary Standards And Also On Satisfying The Criteria Norms Set By Motivational Strips Awards And Recognition Committee (MSARC) And Editorial Board Of SIPAY Journal, Department Of Culture. Government Of Seychelles

Magie Faure - Vidot
Chief Editor - SIPAY

Sabrina Young
Forum Director

Shiju H. Pallithazheth
Founder - Motivational Strips

Jointly Endorsed By

SIPAY
REVUE LITTERAIRE SEYCHELLOISE

NATIONAL PROPERTY OF
DEPARTMENT OF CULTURE. GOVERNMENT OF SEYCHELLES
Literary Journal Of Seychelles Since 2009

Ref: RTMS/22/173
Dtd: 28th May, 2022

Poetic Group

POEMarium

Poetic Parley-105

Pleased to Honour

Fibby Bob Kinney

with

GOLD QUILL

Dr N K Sharma
President

Akshaya K Das
Chief Admn

Dr Dasharath Naik
Vice President

Monica Maartens
Chief Advisor

Since 2017

15 June 2022

Special Mention
Fibby Bob Kinney

Realm of Poems
Paradise of Logophile

Unconditional Love

When is love considered absolute?
When its basis is born upon truth.
When is love considered complete?
When nothing from it you can delete.

Love at its core is a positive trait;
As in the opening of a heavenly gate.
Love is the Diamond forged from coal;
It is created from the fire in the soul.

How do we know when love is absolute?
Like a perfect tune played on a flute.
When is love an unfaltering stance?
As the key to a wholehearted romance.

Is unrestricted love for real?
Within a lovers heart to seal.
A never ending feeling of joy;
Welcomed by both girl and boy.

Unconditional love is the prime goal.
Two hearts entwined to enroll,
With a mission shared by those,
Without the thorns- to be the Rose.

(Fibby Bob Kinney- author)...fBk USA

Thank you; to know more of my work I can be found at rtk922@yahoo.com

Made in the USA
Columbia, SC
17 January 2023

10507124R00171